MW00936310

Faceless

Book Two: The Anonymous Chronicles

———————

Angela Welch Prusia

Amy—
Be the difference!
♥ Angela Welch Prusia
2016

Faceless

The Anonymous Chronicles

Copyright © 2016 by Angela Welch Prusia

Summary: When Josie's father heads to a war zone, she accepts 12 challenges left by the Maj in a yearlong geocache hunt and discovers a friend is battling another war: surviving life on the streets.

Cover: Craig Granger/crowdspring.com
Contact the author: www.angelawelchprusia.com

ISBN 978-1530727476 Paperback
B01E687PKO Kindle

Also by Angela Welch Prusia

BRAiN RIDE

Late Summer Monarch

Tandem

Nameless

For Sarah

Continue to pursue El Roi, the God who sees.

Faceless
The Anonymous Chronicles

Prologue
February 2012

Body odor clung to the old man sleeping on the cardboard mat outside the sandwich shop. The stench mingled with exhaust and diesel fuel from the evening rush hour traffic. Few noticed the homeless man. He blended into the concrete, his presence no more noticeable than the sewer grates.

Bronwyn gaped at the towering buildings around her, sidestepping the faceless individual she only noticed out of the corner of her eye.

"Look." Her sister pointed to the lighted Cinderella carriage across the street. A pair of draft horses clomped against the asphalt, carrying two lovers around the downtown square. "Is she a princess?"

The rare smile on Mama's face warmed Bronwyn's heart, but the moment was short-lived. The homeless man's disgruntled laughter broke the magic. "Fairy tales are dead, little girl."

Kenzie's gaze shifted to the old man who lifted his head off the cardboard. Matted hair peeked from underneath a dingy stocking cap framing a leather face. Street grime caked worn boots.

Bronwyn took a protective step forward, but the man had retreated somewhere inside himself. Bloodshot eyes looked past them. Grey pupils darted back and forth as if searching the distance for something lost.

"Come on." She nudged her sister toward the bus stop.

The old man shifted his weight, muttering a string of indistinguishable words.

Bronwyn couldn't look at Mama. The same fear haunted them both. Life on the run made them vulnerable. How long until they ended up on the streets like the old man?

Chapter One
March 2012

I goosed the throttle and raced after the ATV.

The Maj zigzagged through the trees. He disappeared among the leafy coverage then reappeared like a ghostly apparition on the trail ahead.

Pent-up emotion churned inside me. I hated goodbyes. I hated when the Maj left for Iraq. I hated his second deployment back to the Middle East. Why did he have to leave again?

Twelve months is a lifetime. Especially when you're 14. War wasn't some video game with an on/off switch. What if the Maj got hurt? Worse— what if he didn't come home?

Tears burned my eyes, but I refused to cry. I couldn't lose it. Not now. Even if my goggles hid my tears.

I had to break hard to avoid a collision with the Maj. He idled his ATV at a crossroads in the trail.

"Warn a person." I scowled.

My irritation didn't faze him. "Race you to the river?"

I raised my eyebrows. I never backed down from a challenge. "Loser cleans dishes."

"Deal."

I didn't wait for the countdown.

"Hey, you cheated!" The Maj called out, but I ignored him, surging toward the right and plunging down a ravine. A flock of black birds scattered from the brush.

I pushed harder, closing in on the break in the cottonwood trees. The river peeked through the branches. Water shimmered in the sunlight. Winner was the first to dip the wheels of the ATV into the shallow river.

I hit the sand, kicking up granules that pelted my helmet. One hundred yards to go. I put on a burst of speed, crisscrossing tire tracks from earlier riders.

The Maj leaned forward, trying to gain ground. Neither of us liked to admit defeat, and he was winning by a point after our latest foosball tournament. If something could be won, we kept score, tallying points in our ongoing battle for top dog.

I plowed into the shallows and threw up my arms in victory. "I win! Tie game."

The Maj hit the water a second later, dousing me with cold water. "That's for cheating."

"Whatever!" Water streaked my goggles, but I didn't care. I was half tempted to go for a swim, even though I'd freeze with the early March temps. We were crazy enough to camp in the frosty weather. I wiped the lens with the back of my glove.

"You took off before me." The Maj's protests escalated. Arguing was part of our competitive ritual. Wrangling over points added to the fun.

"Quit whining and congratulate the champ." I pumped my fists and bowed before my imaginary audience.

The Maj laughed, a throaty sound I'd miss when he left. "Congrats, Rooster."

My real name's Josie, but most people call me Rooster. Before my solo days on the ATV, I sat behind the Maj, hugging his waist and getting splattered with mud. A rooster tail marked the backside of every shirt. He christened me with the nickname before I could even remember.

"So we gonna break our tie game before I ship out?"

Blood drained from my face. No matter how much I tried to forget, I couldn't escape reality.

I spun a cookie in the sand. This was my last weekend with my dad for a year.

The Maj joined me, and we went back and forth, making patterns in the sand. I jerked the wheel sharply to the left and whirled around before turning sharply to the right to make a figure eight. Sand landed on my lip.

Tearing around the river bottom always gave me a dizzy rush. I forced my fears aside and lost myself in the fun.

Daylight faded, coloring the sky in pinks and purples. The Maj stopped his ATV and turned in the seat. "Want to head back?"

"Never."

He bit his lip. "Me neither."

I looked away, pretending to look at the water. I. Would. Not. Cry.

"I'm going to miss it." The Maj pulled off his helmet and scanned the landscape, as if memorizing every rock. Every tree. In Afghanistan, he'll work inside a qalat, an earthen fortress located within the perimeter of the FOB (Forward Operating Base).

I studied my dad from the corner of my eye, imprinting his features in my mind. His square jaw. The mole on the back of his neck. The scar on his chin from a bike wreck. The tuft of dark hair that wouldn't stay down. He'll be clean shaven on duty. Not scruffy like today.

"Come on." He returned his helmet then glanced at me before covering his eyes with his goggles. Sadness tinged the light blue pupils.

We took the trail back through the trees toward camp. Branches cracked under our tires, sending a strong wave of pine through my nostrils. Dusk made it hard to see. We were the last two ATVs on the trail.

I ducked to avoid a low-hanging branch. If only I could stall time. I dreaded the farewell ceremony. The airport goodbye.

"Look." The Maj idled his ATV, breaking my thoughts. He pointed ahead.

I craned my neck and saw a doe and her fawn. The last rays of light streamed through the branches and dappled their fur. The doe pricked her ears, but didn't move from the nest under the trees. They were upwind, so neither smelled our scent. The fawn blinked, revealing almond-shaped eyes the color of espresso.

"He's cute, huh?" the Maj whispered.

I wanted to take a picture with my phone. But the shot would be too grainy in the poor light anyway.

We watched the pair in silence. The moment was sacred, a rare glimpse into the secret life hidden among the trees. I imagined the fawn's arrival in the quiet of night and pictured its first shaky steps. Did the fawn look up into the starry night and wonder at the vastness of its new world?

"Ready?" the Maj mouthed before revving the engine.

The doe nudged her fawn as if to say good night. I could stay here forever.

The trail wound through the trees for another mile before I spotted bright yellow canvas. Two pup tents faced a fire pit. Other than an RV parked on the far side of the campground, we were the only other campers. The Maj let me skip school for the day so we could have extra time together.

"I can already taste the steaks." The Maj turned off his ignition and dismounted.

I shook my braid free and noticed the time. We'd been riding for over five hours. No wonder my stomach growled. I walked over to the cooler and rummaged through the ice for something to drink.

The Maj grabbed some newspaper and stoked the fire. Flames grew, rising from the wood.

"Want to grab the meat?"

I pulled the package out of the food cooler and handed it to the Maj. He added his homemade seasoning and dropped two steaks across the metal grate. Something else I'd miss. The Maj was the grill master at home.

"Grrr." He did his manly grunt. "Man loves meat."

I shucked two corn cobs and wrapped them in foil before taking a seat. The Maj positioned the corn on either side of the steaks while I stretched out my legs.

The warmth from the fire made me sleepy. But I couldn't doze off. Not when every minute counted. I wanted each second to stretch for as long as possible. After he left, time could disappear as fast as it did now.

But it wouldn't. Time would drag until his return.

The first time the Maj deployed, I had no concept of time. I was in preschool, so Mom filled a container with red and white peppermints to help me measure time. Each day we ate a mint, counting down the days until his return from Iraq.

The second deployment I was in fourth grade. My chest tightened at the slightest whiff of peppermint. I couldn't stomach the things.

This time, the lump in my throat felt like a boulder ready to crush my every breath. A Sharpie waited by the calendar. Every X would be a reminder of time's irony.

"Someone's deep in thought." The Maj waved his hand in front of my face.

I tucked my legs under me on the lawn chair. "Just wishing you could stay home."

He shook his head. "You know the answer."

I exhaled. The same loyalty which made him a great soldier made him a great father.

"Promise me you'll go easy on your mother." He turned over the steaks. "Don't be difficult."

I frowned. My mom didn't understand me any more than I got her. For one, she refused to camp at anything other than a Hilton.

He narrowed his eyes. "I'm serious. Don't provoke her."

"But . . ."

"No buts." The Maj pulled out camping plates. "Ceasefire starts today."

I started to protest, but he held out his hand. "There's enough fighting in Afghanistan. I don't need combat at home."

Food distracted me. I unwrapped the foil on the corn, and steam wet my face. Butter slid down the golden kernels, making my mouth water.

"This beats MREs in the field." The Maj sliced into his steak, while I stabbed the meat with my fork and lifted it to my lips. I was hungry enough to eat anything—including a shelf-stable meal ready to eat.

Mom would cringe because I didn't bother with a knife, but the Maj ignored my lack of manners. He pulled an envelope from his pocket and handed it to me. "For when I'm gone."

I stopped mid-bite and tore into the envelope. An index card listed a pair of coordinates. "A geocache?"

A grin spread across the Maj's face. He'd been a geocache junkie since he got a GPS for Father's Day. "Are you game?"

Mom didn't understand our treks through nature to find junk, but the Maj got me hooked. I loved the adventure.

Geocaching is basically a treasure hunt on steroids. People—2 million according to one website—hide "caches" or treasures in obscure places around the world.

Me and the Maj have tramped through woods, searched through museums, biked along trails, and navigated unfamiliar cities looking for caches.

The grossest cache we ever found was a fake wad of chewed up gum. The hollow inside held a tiny roll of paper to log our names. The best cache was an ammo can filled with kiddie toys from fast food places. I exchanged a plastic keychain for a flexible Gumby which still sits atop my alarm clock.

I pulled out my phone. Geocaches aren't limited to GPS devices like when the hobby first started. Now there's a downloadable app. "So, you want me to look for the cache now?"

"Tomorrow. It's too dark." He leaned forward, his eyes gleaming. "I've hidden one challenge for every month I'm gone."

A yearlong treasure hunt with challenges. Cool. "Definitely beats the mints."

Our eyes locked, emotion thick. "I hope so."

I turned over the index card and read the clue inked across the back. "Don't be afraid to fly."

I scanned the area, repeating the clue in my head.

Trees ringed the campsite. A walking path meandered past the tent sites toward a covered pavilion filled with picnic tables. A pair of swings on the playground creaked in the slight wind.

When I was a kid, I used to pump my legs on the swings until I was high enough to fly off the seat. Is that what the clue meant?

The Maj played dumb when I asked him for a hint.

I frowned, dumping my plate into the tub of dish water. "Too bad you have dishes."

"Only because I'm a good sport." The Maj grabbed a rag. "Some of us aren't cheaters."

I stuck out my tongue and sat beside the fire, still trying to figure out where the cache could be hidden. Warmth crept through my body, making me drowsy despite my effort to stay awake.

"Don't fall asleep, *chica*," the Maj called out. "We still have s'mores to make."

My eyes fluttered open, but I was too tired to answer. A few minutes later, the Maj shook my foot. "Hey, sleepyhead. Dishes are done. Ready for a marshmallow?"

The fire had died, leaving perfect white embers. He plucked his stick over the heat, while I dunked mine into a last flickering flame. No golden brown marshmallows for me. I liked them charred.

I unwrapped a piece of chocolate and pressed a graham cracker sandwich around my marshmallow. It oozed out of the sides and stuck to my fingers.

The Maj leaned back in his lawn chair and savored his creation.

"So this treasure hunt you devised," I talked with a mouthful. "Is it registered online?"

He shook his head. "It's your own private treasure hunt."

11

I blinked, touched that he'd done this for me. "What if I can't find all the caches?"

He yawned. "You will. Believe in yourself."

I wanted the same confidence, but I'd be a wreck if I couldn't find one of the Maj's caches. It was disappointing enough when we couldn't locate a geocache together.

"Ready to call it a night?" The Maj dumped the dishwater onto the dying flames, sending a plume of black smoke billowing upward.

I didn't feel like trekking to the bathroom, so I brushed my teeth using a water bottle, then found a tree to relieve myself. The Maj had already crawled into his tent.

"Good night," he called out when I unzipped my tent.

"'Night." I lingered at the opening until I heard his regular breathing. The Maj never took long to fall asleep.

I grabbed my flashlight.

I had a geocache to find.

***

"This is your first night, isn't it?" Ms. Carmen, the director of the mission, asked. A shock of short white hair contrasted with skin the color of toffee. Wrinkles made her eyes smile.

Bronwyn resisted the urge to sniff her armpits. Did they already smell like the streets?

Mama straightened her shoulders. "Is it that obvious?"

"Your eyes betray the truth." Ms. Carmen didn't pretend life was perfect. "You're terrified and confused."

Bronwyn looked down. *Vulnerability destroyed their chances of survival. Life on the run demanded certain rules be followed. Trust no one. Always have an escape plan. Show no fear.*

Mama scanned the room at the shelter. Twelve metal bunkbeds lined dingy walls devoid of color. Scuff marks crisscrossed the linoleum. The place smelled like body odor and desperation. She lifted the corner of a thin grey mattress to check for bed bugs. "It's been a long three months. We're just tired."

Bronwyn didn't want to remember the nights huddling in the Corolla to keep warm. Finding an apartment without a deposit had been impossible. Christmas had blurred into the string of days rooted to nowhere.

Ms. Carmen narrowed dark brown eyes. "I'm not here to pry." The woman handed them each a worn blanket and a flat pillow. "We have resources at the mission if you want help."

Bronwyn kept quiet. She and Kenzie knew better than to defy Mama and talk about their situation. Sleeping at the shelter was hard enough to accept.

Ms. Carmen walked past the bunkbeds toward a communal bathroom. Disinfectant didn't mask the underlying stench. An adjoining room mirrored the room where they stood. Twelve metal bunkbeds cramped the tight space already filling with bodies for the night. "Doors close at nine. First come, first serve."

Bronwyn crawled into the top bunk, exhausted. She tried not to think about standing in line every night for a bed.

Reality hit like a hard slap across the face.

They were homeless.

Chapter Two

Grey clouds shrouded the moon as I headed for the trees. The stillness magnified the call of spring peepers. The same loud silence filled the house at night whenever the Maj left. The low buzz of the refrigerator. The whir of our ceiling fan. The creak of a loose floorboard in the kitchen. The lonely groans of an empty house always exaggerated his absence.

Light from my flashlight bobbed in a circle in front of me. The air smelled heavy with the coming storm.

The GPS pointed to the left, near the RV, so I walked toward that direction. Something flew at my head.

"Ugh!" I shrieked without thinking.

"Who's there?" a voice called out of the camper, making my heart jump.

I froze. Maybe wandering around the dark wasn't such a brilliant idea.

A light turned on inside the RV. Someone fumbled with the door knob. I ducked into the shadows to hide.

A man with bushy hair and flannels searched the dark. A white t-shirt stretched over his beer belly.

"Must be some critter, Vera," he called out to an unseen person inside the camper. I prayed his voice didn't carry. Combat made the Maj a light sleeper.

I waited a full five minutes after the light turned off. Thankfully the Maj didn't stir, and the RV people settled back to sleep. My heart slowed, so I left the shadows and moved toward the trees.

I was close according to the GPS. Coordinates point to the general location of the geocache. Then comes the fun—the hunt.

I aimed the light on the nearest branch, and a bead of sap gleamed. I ran the light along the bark. Nothing out of the ordinary caught my eye, so I moved to the next tree. I blinded a sleepy squirrel tucked in a hole. We both jumped back in surprise. It chattered at me, defending her home. I held my breath, hoping the RV guy didn't come out brandishing a weapon.

Try explaining geocaching to a guy with a gun—I'd probably pee my pants.

A droplet of rain landed on my cheek. Another hit my head. I didn't want to give up. But I didn't want to get caught in a rain shower either.

My squirrel friend burrowed back into its hole, so I decided to do the same. I could return in the morning. More rain splattered my head, so I hurried through the undergrowth. My foot snagged a root, and I stumbled to the ground.

"Ouch," I cursed under my breath. Blood oozed through the dirt on my knee. I swiped my hand across the exposed skin and winced at the sting. I was such a klutz.

My flashlight rolled past my reach. Something rustled in the brush, making my head jerk toward the sound. An awful smell assaulted me. Beady eyes gleamed at me, piercing the dark. The animal walked into the beam of light.

My eyes widened in fear. A streak of white fur stood out from a pelt of black. A skunk ambled toward me as if taunting me.

I backed up slowly, using my hands like the crab walk. Pine needles dug into my flesh, but I hardly

15

noticed. I couldn't get sprayed. Mom would bathe me in tomato sauce and ban me from the airport farewell.

A bolt of lightning flashed above me, illuminating the sky. A clap of thunder followed, scaring me as much as the skunk. The animal scurried under the trees. Time to make my getaway. I jumped to my legs and dashed for the tent.

Rain pelted the canvas moments after I zipped up the door. I kicked off my shoes and fell back on my sleeping bag in relief. Good thing the Maj was asleep. Otherwise, he wouldn't let me live down my run-in with the skunk.

Storms didn't scare me. I loved the feel of the rising tempo like an orchestra tuning up before a concert.

I climbed into my mummy bag, and watched the shadows of the overhanging branches cast eerie shapes above me. The creak of their grizzly forms reminded me of the scary stories the girls and I swapped at sleepovers. If it weren't for Teegan, Bing, Mia, and Hoot, I'd never survive the days without the Maj. We'd been best friends since the day we met on the basketball court at the YMCA as kids.

My eyes drooped as the wind lulled me to sleep. I woke up to rain pelting my tent like a machine gun. The Maj called my name above a howling gust.

"Rooster? You okay?"

"Yeah." I wiped the sleep from my eyes. It felt like I'd only slept five minutes. Water seeped into my tent at the seam. The edge of my pillow was soaked.

"We need to leave. We're in a tornado watch."

I shuddered. My aunt's house was reduced to a pile of wood after a twister hit. The town was still rebuilding two years later.

"Put on your shoes," he yelled over the rain. "We need to find shelter."

A tree branch splintered outside, spurring me faster. I unzipped my tent and got a face full of water.

The Maj grabbed my hand, and we dashed for the truck. Lightning lit up the sky while thunder boomed.

I jumped into the passenger seat and pulled the door shut. Water pooled on the seat around me. The clock on the dash read 4:55.

"Let's get out of here." The Maj blasted the cab with heat and tore through the camp like a crazy man. "There's a café a mile away. Let's hope the farmers like their coffee early."

I shivered.

"There should be a blanket in back."

I unbuckled my seatbelt and rustled around the seat until I felt fleece. Wrapping its warmth around me took off the chill from my wet clothes.

We pulled into town a minute later. Rain blurred the three-digit number on the green population sign. 609? 804? You could blink and miss Main Street. No 24-hour Walmarts in this Podunk town. Not one car lined the street. Not good.

We drove past a bank and the community center as a light flipped on inside Grammie's Café. Employees probably parked around back.

"Bingo." The Maj pulled next to the handicapped stall. "Let's grab breakfast and wait out the storm."

I loved breakfast outdoors, especially when the Maj used his cast iron skillet to make pancakes and bacon. But even if the rain stopped, sitting in cold puddles of water didn't sound fun.

We dashed for the door only to find it locked. Three minutes till opening. The Maj pounded on the glass.

An older woman with shoulder-length grey hair glided toward us. She wore a fitted t-shirt and yoga pants. The smell of coffee and cinnamon spilled from the restaurant when she opened the door.

"Come in." The woman let her glasses fall to the chain holding them and eyed us. Her nametag read, Grammie.

"Thank you," the Maj gushed. "We didn't want to get caught in our tent if the storm gets worse."

"Figured as much. Nobody's a stranger around here."

We followed her to a booth in the corner. "Make yourselves comfortable." She grabbed an apron hanging on a hook and tied it around her small waist. "I'll get you some menus."

I surveyed the cozy space filled with Americana décor. If a tornado hit, the place would be flattened.

"We got us a cellar if the sirens go off." She read my mind. Grammie set down the menus and poured the Maj coffee. "How about some hot cocoa, young lady?"

"Please." I scanned the specials.

"Did you see the cinnamon rolls?" The Maj nodded toward a display case.

"Whoa." My eyes bugged out at the size of the rolls wrapped in plastic wrap. "Wanna split one?"

The Maj nodded. "Sounds good—with a couple fried eggs and some bacon."

I closed the menu. It was easy to order with the Maj. My mom didn't touch meat or sugar—my personal favorites.

"Hope you're not in a hurry." Grammie set down my cocoa and pulled out a notepad. "My cook's stuck at home with a downed power line, so it's just me until my other waitress arrives."

"No rush." The Maj ordered our food. "We're not moving until the rain lets up."

I blew on my hot cocoa while Grammie disappeared behind the counter. The chocolate surface rippled with my breath. Outside, the storm raged stronger.

"I'm so glad we're inside." The Maj cupped his hands around his mug and took a long sip of coffee.

"Think the tents will blow away?" My taste buds melted at the taste.

Memory made the Maj smile. "Wouldn't be the first time."

I leaned back in my chair. I'd heard the story enough to recite, but I didn't care. I'd listen to a hundred stories—anything to lengthen our time together.

"Poppy and me got caught in a thunderstorm one morning out on the lake when we were fishing. Out of nowhere, this tent somersaulted in front of us and skidded into the water." The Maj laughed. "Turns out, the tent was ours."

"So, what'd you do?" I already knew the answer.

"Poppy and me stripped down to our boxers before we remembered we couldn't swim." The Maj grinned. "The next day, Poppy signed all five of us kids up for swimming lessons."

I stifled a laugh, and a hiccup escaped. "In case you ever had to swim after flyaway tents?"

We both laughed when Grammie arrived with our food. Thick white frosting laced the top of my cinnamon roll.

19

"Let me know if you need anything else." Grammie walked toward the window and gazed at the sky. "My regular coffee crew won't venture out till after the storm."

Halfway through my roll, the tornado sirens screamed to action. I stuffed the last strip of bacon into my mouth and followed Grammie and the Maj down the cement stairs to the cellar. Cold air made goose bumps rise on my arms.

"Hold tight till I find the chain for the light." Grammie disappeared into the darkness. Nothing fazed her. The woman had to be pushing 70. She was fearless.

Light flooded the room, revealing cement walls. At least we were safe down here.

"Anyone up for Dutch Blitz?" Grammie pulled out a stack of cards from a plastic tub filled with blankets. Apparently this wasn't the first time Grammie had waited out a tornado.

"Never played." The Maj handed me a blanket, and I spread it over the floor, careful to avoid a large spider web in the corner.

Turned out Grammie was a card shark. The woman was more competitive than me and the Maj combined. She won five games before we took a break, but at least it wasn't the Maj winning. Our running competition was still tied after my ATV win.

"So, you from around here?" The Maj stretched his legs.

"New England actually. Daddy got killed in the war, so I had to quit school to help Mama with the kids while she worked."

I didn't know what to say. Kids at school always said stupid stuff about the Maj leaving. It wouldn't be so bad if we lived on an Army post, but we were surrounded by civilians. No one really understood the sacrifices made by part-time soldiers in the National Guard.

"Hardship builds character." Grammie sighed. "You buck up or get bitter. No one likes a whiner."

The Maj squeezed my hand, but it didn't alleviate my fears.

Grammie didn't miss our exchange. "You leaving with the 734th?"

The Maj nodded.

"My grandson's in your group." She held his gaze. "Name's Harrison."

The Maj's raised his eyebrows. "Tall kid. Good head on his shoulders."

Pride shone in Grammie's smile. "Can you keep an eye out for him?"

The Maj's lips tightened. He never talked about it, but I knew responsibility for his soldiers weighed heavy. "You have my word."

The cellar suddenly felt like a tomb as silence settled around us. Fear tightened a hand around my throat. Bombings. Terrorists. Hostages. Beheadings. Fragments of news headlines pummeled my brain. I couldn't breathe.

"Grammie?" Footsteps sounded on the stairs.

I straightened, gulping in air.

"Katrina?" Grammie squeaked.

"Thank goodness you're alright." A young woman stood in the doorway, her blonde hair pulled back in a ponytail. A grey shirt stretched across her bulging stomach. "I got scared when you weren't in the kitchen."

Grammie hugged the woman. "Me? You got a baby to worry about."

21

"Storm's over." She grinned. "And you need help. The restaurant's full."

Grammie jumped to action. "I gotta run. Meet Katrina," she called over her shoulder as she dashed up the cellar steps. "She and my grandson are going to have my first great grandchild."

Harrison?

Steely resolve lit the Maj's eyes. Harrison would become a father on the battlefield.

We hurried to make introductions as we followed Katrina back up the cement stairs.

"Sorry to be rude." She stood at the kitchen door. "I'd love to chat, but we got hungry mouths to feed."

The restaurant was crawling with half the town. We got a box for the rest of the cinnamon roll and walked outside where people talked in groups and surveyed the damage. The sun rose in the east, revealing the destruction. A tornado missed the town, but the high winds had wreaked havoc. Tree limbs littered the ground. Water droplets beaded broken window glass, sparkling like crystal—an ironic display of beauty amidst the mess.

The Maj and I looked at each other.

"Ready to do damage control?"

I nodded, wondering what—if anything—would be left back at camp.

***

"Whoa." I opened the truck, and my tennis shoes sunk into mud. One of our tents sprawled flat against the ground, its poles snapped in half. The other was a twisted mess of canvas tangled among the lowest branches of a cottonwood tree. "All this from high winds?"

"Crazy, huh?" The Maj blinked. "Good thing we left."

I walked over to our cooler which had overturned, and picked up a bottle of ketchup and two cans of Dr. Pepper. A raven swooped down to snag a stray tortilla chip. The empty bag was long gone—along with the rest of our food. Good thing we had breakfast at Grammie's.

"Salvage what we can. Toss the rest." The Maj flung a soggy tennis shoe into the truck bed. It hit the metal and echoed in the quiet after the storm.

Cold droplets dripped from my pillow. Water weighted my mummy bag. Trying to heave it over the side of the truck got me a fresh drenching. A hot shower would feel so good.

Thirty minutes later, we were ready to leave when the Maj remembered the geocache. I'd completely forgotten.

I bit my lip. The GPS could be anywhere. "Uh, we might have a problem." I told him about my adventure in the dark.

The Maj was amused. "A skunk?"

I flashed a toothy smile.

We found the GPS inside my duffle bag. Apparently I'd tucked it inside my bag before falling asleep. I couldn't believe it was actually dry and working.

The Maj leaned against the truck. "Remember the clue?"

Something about flying. I sidestepped a big puddle and headed for the trees. The light made the search easier. A bird's nest caught my eye. The twigs were too uniform—like something from a craft

23

store. I leaned closer and saw a wire attaching the fake nest to the branch. No birds here. Or white poo. My hand touched a thin tube resting at the bottom.

"Found it!" A tingle of excitement coursed through me. I resisted the urge to open the container. If I dropped something in the brush, it would be hard to find.

"It's about time," the Maj teased me when I returned to the truck. "I almost fell asleep."

I climbed into the passenger side and turned the tube over in my hand. Flecks of olive green spray paint dotted my skin. I spilled the contents onto my lap. A small piece of paper was rolled into a scroll and secured with a rubber band.

"Just a log?" Disappointment laced my voice. Most caches had a log to record the dates and names of those who made the discovery. I hoped for something more. Even a stupid kiddie toy would beat this.

"Unroll it."

I snapped off the rubber band. The strip of paper was thin, but long. It curled around my finger until I flattened it to read three numbers. 36, 5, 19.

My eyebrows knit in concentration.

"The combination for my foot locker." His eyes glinted with mystery. "You'll find the first challenge there."

I memorized the numbers in case I lost the slip of paper.

"There's one condition." The Maj drummed his fingers against the steering wheel. "You have to wait to open the foot locker until I'm gone."

I slumped into the seat. The Maj was trying to ease the painful goodbye, but the reminder only stung. "Can we go now?"

The Maj looked disappointed at my lack of excitement, but I couldn't pretend. My emotions were already a mess.

***

Bronwyn rolled onto her back. Water stained the ceiling panels above her, leaving behind a yellow-brown trail snaking across the room. She could touch the ceiling with her fingertips. It pressed against her body like a vice.

She hated the top bunk, but it was better than a mat on the floor. When the temperatures dipped and the beds ran out, people slept on mats, cramming into every possible inch of floor space.

Tonight 30 bodies sucked the same oxygen, slowly suffocating Bronwyn. She'd never get used to the clash of body odors. Each night brought a new stream of faceless people— battered wives, kids, addicts, disabled people, unemployed veterans. Every person had a story.

A woman with a cobra tattoo snored across the room. Her oldest daughter lashed out at anyone who looked at her wrong. The youngest wet her bed. Urine soiled the sheets and saturated the air.

Bronwyn shifted, and the lump under the flat pillow poked her in the head. If only she didn't have to sleep with her backpack, but Ms. Carmen warned them to sleep with their belongings. Shoes were no different. Sleeping in socks was a luxury they couldn't afford. Not if they wanted shoes in the morning.

She stared at the ceiling, trying to suppress the scream that wanted to erupt.

Happy thoughts. Bronwyn forced herself to dwell on the good memories spent with her friends on the basketball court. She wished she had a picture of the girls tucked inside her bag.

Bronwyn squeezed her eyes shut and imagined her friends—the ones she'd left when they'd escaped three months earlier. The unlikely friendship had formed despite her attempt to distance herself from the girls on her basketball team. Fleeing was easier without painful goodbyes.

Rooster was the power forward on their team. Her passion for the outdoors came from her father, a major in the Army National Guard. Bronwyn wondered if he'd left for Afghanistan yet.

Mia, shooting guard, and the fashionista of the team could transform rags into an outfit made for models. Long ebony hair and a flawless bronze complexion made her a beauty with the brains to match.

Brittany, or Bing, brought fun to any situation with her mess of red curls and bubbly personality. The point guard on the team, she was a double-shot of energy espresso who only slowed down when engrossed with an art project.

Small forward Holly, a.k.a. Hoot, loved all things furry or feathered. Her volunteer work at the animal shelter took up every minute she wasn't on the basketball court. The zoo at her home no doubt increased by a potbellied pig when Bing's neighbor, Larry, the old Vietnam vet, had died. Hoot would adopt Jellybean before letting him suffer any more trauma after his owner's death.

And Teegan, her former rival, had proven to have a heart to match her height. When Teegan discovered Bronwyn was running from her abusive father, she'd given up winning the season's last game to help.

A tear leaked down Bronwyn's face. Missing her friends hurt more than the hunger, more than the fear of her father, more than the uncertainty of life on the run.

Here in the dark, Bronwyn didn't have to be strong. She gave into the tears and cried until fatigue finally came.

Chapter Three

Puke threatened to erupt from me like last year's science fair volcano. I pushed aside my breakfast. I couldn't eat.

The Maj's rucksack waited by the door. He'd go with the advance party. The rest of the soldiers would follow within the week.

I stuck in my headphones, but kept the volume low. Music kept the panic attacks at bay, but I didn't want to miss the sound of the Maj's voice—even if he and Mom were talking mundane travel details.

When they finished, the Maj patted Petey's head. Our Great Dane could sense something was wrong. He licked the Maj's hand and whimpered at the door when we climbed into Mom's hybrid. Petey acted the same way the day my older brother Colter left for boot camp.

I stared out the window, counting down the mile markers to the airport. Rush hour traffic had passed, so we arrived in record time. Unfortunately.

We walked in silence through the terminal. Mom clung to the Maj, her eyes puffy from crying. If only Colter could've made the send-off, but he was away at Airborne School. I dreaded the day they both got sent on deployments at the same time.

People swirled around us, largely oblivious to our circumstances. A few people took notice of the uniform and nodded in gratitude. One guy with long hair even called out a hearty, "Thanks, man."

I wondered about the flight connections these strangers would make. A business conference? A trip to see grandparents? A vacation to the beach? I wished we could be so lucky. But our world revolved in another orbit. Deployment.

Because of Homeland Security, we could only go as far as the security checkpoint.

"I guess this is it." The Maj stopped near a newspaper kiosk out of the flow of traffic. I tried to ignore the glaring headlines. *Six missing British soldiers presumed dead after an explosion in southwest Afghanistan.*

We huddled in a circle.

"Make sure to write." He stalled. "Mail from my girls is gold."

I could only nod. My throat burned from the lump of emotions blocking my airway.

The Maj handed me a set of dog tags. "Your name is on one tag, and mine is on the other."

I traced my fingers against the raised letters. "Thanks." I clasped the chain around my neck and tucked the tags under my t-shirt so they rested against my heart. The metal was cold against my flesh, but I wouldn't take them off until the Maj returned home.

"Tie game until I return." He bumped my fist and pulled me into his embrace.

I inhaled the rugged smell of the Maj combined with the faintest whiff of his cologne. I wanted to melt into his strong arms.

"I have to leave," he whispered and gently pulled away from me.

My arms hung limply at my side. I immediately felt his absence. I bit my lip while my parents held each other and then kissed before tearing apart.

"See ya," the Maj said in a gruff voice meant to disguise his emotions. He turned quickly and walked down the corridor. Mom hugged her arms around her torso.

I wanted to run after him. Anything to relieve the pressure. My lungs felt like they would explode.

His camouflage disappeared from sight.

I would hate airports until the day I died.

***

Mom didn't have to work at the hospital, so she let me play hooky from school. We headed to the closest theater and drowned our emotions in a comedy and a tub of large popcorn—extra butter. Afterwards, Mom wanted a pedicure, so I let her drag me into the nail salon. I unlaced my combat boots and asked for camouflage polish. Mom leaned back into the massage chair and held her tongue. Twelve months together without the Maj or Colter to break up our battles might kill us both.

When we finally headed home, Mom got lost in a book, and I headed for our unfinished basement. The chill made me shiver as I passed my brother's weight equipment. The Maj's foot locker was pushed into the crawl space underneath the stairs.

I crouched to avoid hitting my head on a beam and ate a cobweb. I spit out the sticky thread and grabbed the handle on the foot locker. It scraped along the cement floor when I pulled the black container onto the large carpet remnant in the main room.

The overhead bulb illuminated William Wallace's freedom speech from *Braveheart* which was taped to the top of the foot locker. The Maj and I had watched the movie so many times, our DVD copy needed replacing.

Tears welled in my eyes, making the numbers on the combination lock swim in my vision. 36, 5, 19. I twisted the black face until the latch popped. The lid lifted easily in my hand.

The faint smell of pine filled my nose as I peered inside. The box was empty except for a single stack of envelopes bound with a rubber band.

I thumbed through the pile of challenges—one for each month. Twelve words in the Maj's familiar scrawl were inked across the front of each sealed envelope.

Miracles. Dare. Together. Death. Regret. Procrastination. Catalyst. Distractions. Courage. Passion. Anyway. Legacy.

I traced my fingers over the word "miracle" on the first envelope and imagined the Maj writing each clue. He was a leftie like me.

I returned the other envelopes and hurried upstairs to find Petey. "Want to go for an adventure?"

My partner in crime lifted his head from the couch and cocked an ear.

"My guess is that we'll find the first cache in the dog park since the clue said to search your favorite spot."

Petey wagged his tail.

"I figured you'd be excited." I raised my eyebrows. "Think Lucy will be there?"

I swear Petey reddened. He'd been sweet on the Goldendoodle since her owner moved into the neighborhood six months earlier.

I grabbed a pullover I'd gotten from one of the recruiters in the Maj's office, and we headed out the door.

Petey pulled on his leash before I could press the keypad on the garage. "Hold on, Romeo. We don't even know if Lucy will be at the dog park."

31

Her name only excited him more.

"So much for a leisurely stroll, huh?"

We took the shortcut to the dog park. Petey nearly took off my arm when he spotted Lucy and made a beeline for the gate.

I couldn't help but laugh as I lifted the latch. My dog was a hopeless romantic.

A half dozen dogs of various breeds ran around the grassy acreage enclosed by a chain link fence. Lucy's owner, a woman with two small kids, greeted Petey when he bounded toward them.

"Can you tell he's happy to see you?" I called out, careful to step out of the way of a guy throwing a Frisbee to his Mastiff. The dog leapt for the disk, saliva raining off his chops. I wasn't in the mood for a bath of slobber.

I pulled out my GPS, careful not to draw attention. True cachers avoided detection. They steered clear of revealing their secrets to muggles, a term borrowed from the Harry Potter books to describe non-geocachers.

"Where are you?" I muttered to myself as I scanned the fence line. A clump of pine trees seemed like the most obvious place.

Petey and Lucy trotted up to me.

"Hey, girl." I stroked Lucy's soft fur. "Want to play fetch with me and Petey?"

I swear my dog rolled his eyes. Apparently he wanted alone time with his girl. Lucy trumped me any day of the week.

"What?" I tried to entice Petey with the ball I'd brought. "Impress your girl with your athletic prowess." I leaned down to whisper in his ear. "Girls love macho."

My pep talk had the desired effect. Petey leaned on his haunches, poised for me to fling the ball.

"That a way, boy. Go get it." I flung the ball toward the trees.

Petey darted for the ball, so I took off after him, and Lucy followed. No one would notice anything out of the ordinary if I engaged Petey and Lucy in a game of catch.

I disappeared behind the first tree, my breath ragged from my burst of speed. A bird squawked at my intrusion. Three blind babies arched their bald heads upward out of their nest, beaks open for food.

"Sorry guys," I rasped. "Didn't mean to interrupt lunchtime."

Petey dropped the ball in front of Lucy like a bouquet of flowers. She wagged her tail and nuzzled close to him.

"Okay, you two lovebirds." I launched the ball in the air. "Who's faster?" The dogs took off, and I checked the GPS.

I'd guessed right. The cache was within reach.

My gaze narrowed on the fence. The perfect place for a magnet. I ran my hand along the underside of the top bar and made contact with a micro cache the size of a bolt head.

"Sneaky, Maj," I muttered under my breath and smiled. I was lucky to find such a hard cache so quickly. I twisted off the top and pulled out a thin strip of paper rolled into the small space.

"I know you're worried about my safety, but don't forget to live while I'm gone. Challenge #1: Find the miracles around you."

A tear leaked down my face as I left the trees. I should have brought my shades. The last thing I

33

wanted was to have an emotional meltdown at the dog park.

Lucy trotted up to me with the ball.

"Good girl." I couldn't help but crack a smile. Lucy wouldn't let a Great Dane show her up. The girl had spirit.

Petey sensed my mood and cocked his head with that knowing look.

"I'll be okay." I hugged his neck, inhaling the mix of grass and dog sweat. "I just miss the Maj." Petey licked my cheek, and the rough texture of his tongue made me smile.

"Thanks," I whispered. "Did you know you were a miracle?"

Lucy joined in, and she and Petey drenched me in slobber. So much for wanting to avoid a saliva bath. Dog drool dripped off me.

***

"Is she in there?" A hand waved in front of my face. "Earth to Rooster."

I blinked, and details rushed at me. Laughter. Sound bites from a dozen conversations. The musky scent of Mia's perfume. My camouflage backpack flung onto the cafeteria table. Four sets of eyeballs peering into mine. Strange how you can be surrounded by people and still feel so alone.

My friends leaned over the table. They were so close, I could smell the menu on their collective breath—spaghetti and garlic bread.

"Standby, folks." Teegan's familiar voice reached my ears. "We have contact. The subject appears to be waking from her catatonic state."

Bing lunged for me, wrapping my neck in a strong embrace. Her mass of red curls pushed my dog tags into my flesh, no doubt imprinting the Maj's name into my skin.

"Don't choke the girl." Mia hooked her finger around Bing's belt and yanked her off me.

"Sorry." Bing plopped down on her seat and nearly fell off the bench. "We just missed you at school yesterday."

"You're going to get through this." Hoot shifted her weight, and the braids on her weave swayed. If she could smuggle something furry into her pocket like a gerbil to make me smile, she would. A similar stunt in elementary got her sent home for the rest of the day.

I nodded, absently twirling spaghetti noodles with my fork. I'd been a wreck all morning. If it weren't for the girls pulling me to class, I'd be slumped against my locker, unable to move.

Bing pulled her sketchpad from her backpack. "I have something for you." She opened to a watercolor painting that made my jaw drop.

"Whoa," Hoot gasped. "It looks just like Rooster and the Maj."

I couldn't take my eyes off Bing's gift. Few people saw past the whirlwind of motion to the artist who could capture emotions with the touch of a brushstroke. A watercolor which hung over Teegan's bed revealed the protective love Teegan felt for her little sister who lived in a world of silence.

"You have some serious talent, girl." Mia shook her head in amazement.

When I tried to find words to thank Bing, she got as red as her hair.

"We're all here for you." Teegan reached for a fist bump before the moment got awkward. "You hurt, we all hurt."

I managed a weak smile. Anything more and my emotions would spill out in a blubbery mess of snot and hiccups.

"Have you heard from the Maj?" Mia's ebony eyes pooled with compassion.

I could only shake my head. Waiting was the hardest.

"New subject." Teegan could see my discomfort. "Are you going to the pizza party tonight?"

The thought of celebrating turned my stomach, even if we had won the final club basketball tournament. How could I party if the Maj was in danger?

"You're not going to crawl into a hole for the next 12 months." Mia wagged a manicured nail at me. "We'll drag you to the party, kicking and screaming."

"Don't mess with the girls." Bing flashed me a smile. "Trust me. They don't give up." She didn't have to mention her hospital stay 18 months earlier when she was on suicide watch. The girls had stuck by Bing until she emerged from the darkness after her parents' divorce.

"Okay," I caved. "You win. I'll go."

Cheers erupted around me.

"So, what are we going to do now that club season is over?" Mia asked.

I couldn't bring myself to tell the girls about the geocache hunt. Call me selfish, but I wanted my dad all to myself. In some strange way, the caches would bridge the distance and connect us.

"Help at the shelter," Hoot piped up.

"To see the animals or Collin?" Bing teased. Hoot's boyfriend volunteered as a dog walker.

Hoot wadded up her napkin and tossed it across the table. Bing ducked, and it skidded across the floor.

"Better be careful," Teegan warned. "Trust me. You don't want in-school suspension."

Bing stifled her laughter. Last semester Teegan spent a week in ISS after a food fight—all because a new girl named Bronwyn Keller moved to town and threatened Teegan's position on the basketball team.

"I wonder where Bronwyn's living now," Mia voiced the question which plagued each of us. Bronwyn and her mother and sister had spent the last four years moving from place to place to hide from their abusive father/husband.

Hoot sighed, revealing her braces. "If only she could write us another letter. I miss her so much."

Bronwyn had risked trouble just to send us one letter. We'd scoured the words for the slightest clue to her whereabouts, but even the postage mark meant little. Three months had passed. Bronwyn could be anywhere.

Teegan shifted her tray. "Savanah misses Kenzie. She keeps signing me questions."

Bronwyn's little sister hit it off with Teegan's sister. Even though Kenzie didn't know sign language, the two girls seemed to have a language all their own.

Bing stabbed a meatball. "If I was rich, I'd hire a private investigator. That creep of a dad needs to go to jail."

None of us wanted to remember Bronwyn's narrow escape during our last game, especially since Bronwyn's father had evaded the police.

Had they found an apartment? Did Bronwyn's mother get another waitressing job? Did they have food to eat?

I stared at the untouched food on my tray. Ever since Teegan's work with Campus Kitchen gave her a personal look at hunger, she usually said something when we wasted food. Today she said nothing about my waste. Obviously my mental state was too fragile.

The bell rang, but I didn't move. I checked my phone again—even though I knew there would be no word from the Maj. It was a habit I had to break. Simple texts were no longer a luxury.

Mia dumped my tray, and Hoot pulled me to my feet. She might be the petite one on our starting lineup, but working with the large dogs at the animal shelter made her strong. That and her new pet, Jellybean. Watching her wrestle the potbellied pig in an effort to train him to obey commands was a hoot—just like her nickname.

"Come on, Rooster." The girls dragged me down the hall. "Let's get you to class."

What would I do without my friends? I could barely focus on what subject I had next.

***

I changed into pajamas after the pizza party and crawled under the jungle netting that hung over my bed. Petey sprawled out beside me, hogging all but a corner of my camouflage blanket.

"Get comfortable, why don't you?" I nudged his big head. I swore my Great Dane thought he was a lap dog.

He flung out his paw in answer.

38

"Very funny." I made more room for his massive body and booted up my laptop. Time for my nightly ritual. The Maj loved getting emails from home when he could access the internet. I would send a real letter over the weekend. Mail call was the highlight of his week, and Mom and I loved to spoil the Maj with letters and packages from home.

The screen flashed, casting a bluish light in the dark. I logged into my email account and began my first of many emails.

Hey Maj,

I found the first geocache yesterday. Thirty more days till the next one. Ugh.

Mom and I mailed you and Colter each a care package of homemade cookies. I spent half a day making both your favorites— oatmeal scotchies and chocolate chip.

The girls dragged me to the club pizza party at Coach's house tonight. And even though I hate to admit being wrong, I had fun.

Of course the night wasn't complete without a Bing moment. After the award ceremony, she swung her medal into the punch. Red liquid rained over Coach's husky. The dog shook his fur and speckled the carpet in red. Guess who gets to be Coach's maid this weekend?

We played dodgeball in the dark that morphed into a large-scale battle. Somebody brought out some glow sticks, and kids all over the neighborhood jumped into the fun.

We were dodging balls left and right because all you could see were thin neon bands of color and dark silhouettes.

I think we started an annual tradition. The girls are already talking about buying glow-in-the-dark dodgeballs. Funny, huh?

Miss you like crazy, and we still have 11 more geocaches to go.

Signing off,
Rooster

***

Bronwyn clutched her tray and scanned the school cafeteria at her latest school. Was this the sixth or seventh move in four years? They never stuck around long enough to keep track.

Flashes of memory mixed with the new faces. A girl who looked like Hoot. A hairstyle that Mia would love. A laugh that reminded her of Bing.

No one even glanced her way.

She sighed and picked her way through the mass of bodies. Several kids stood in line at the snack bar recklessly spending their money without a second thought. None of them worried about their next meal or where they would sleep for the night. They didn't panic when they needed a poster for a school project that cost less than a dollar.

Her own heart had dropped when her history teacher announced the assignment during second period. Bronwyn had seen the hollow look in Mama's eyes. Finding work without an address wasn't easy. After filling out two dozen applications, Mama still didn't have a job.

Bronwyn settled for a vacant table near the door. Escape was always best planned ahead. She sat with her back to the wall so she could get a better feel for the layout of the territories.

Becoming invisible was easier when you knew who sat where and what tables should be avoided.

She tucked her apple into her backpack. Saving food had become a habit for the days when food was scare. Bronwyn opened her milk carton with a trembling hand and wished she could blend into the walls. Last time Bronwyn sat alone in a middle school cafeteria, she'd ended up in ISS after a food fight with Teegan Miller.

Bronwyn pulled a notebook from her bag and flipped halfway through the pages to a blank sheet of paper. She took a bite of lasagna and uncapped her pen. If only the girls weren't separated by hundreds of miles.

Mama said mail was too dangerous, but maybe she could beg Ms. Carmen for a stamp if she kept the letter simple. Details left clues. And clues led to trails. She couldn't put Mama or Kenzie at risk.

Bronwyn touched her pen to the paper. She missed the girls something awful. Every memory triggered thoughts of them. Midnight basketball, sleepovers, a snowball fight, junk food potlucks, and spicy milkshakes.

She smiled, remembering the spicy milkshake concoction that cemented her membership into the group. The good luck ritual was a pre-game tradition. Bronwyn closed her eyes, and felt the presence of her friends. Too bad they couldn't connect through social media. But that was another big negative.

The bell broke her thoughts. She stared at the blank piece of paper. As much as Bronwyn wanted to write another letter, she couldn't threaten her family. He was too dangerous.

"Sorry, girls. I just can't do it," Bronwyn whispered before realizing she spoke out loud. She shut the notebook and felt her cheeks redden.

If word got out that she talked to imaginary people, she'd be branded a loser for sure. Life in this new place would be torture.

41

Chapter Four

"Is that a smile?" Teegan poked me in the ribs Friday night.

My attempt to hide behind a can of Mountain Dew didn't work.

"You know we won't let you miss out on our weekly ritual." Bing pelted me with a handful of popcorn. "Even alternating weekends between my parents doesn't keep me from our sleepovers."

"She's right." Hoot hugged her knees. "We made a pact a long time ago. No one misses Friday night sleepovers unless you're puking or dead."

Posters of fashion models peeked from between two bookcases lined with books. Mia's room reflected the Mia everyone saw and the studious side only us girls knew. My fears were unfounded. I didn't have to look around our tangle of bodies sitting on her white shag carpet to know there were no secrets between us. If I woke up screaming from a nightmare, my friends would understand.

They never laughed at me for sleeping with Riley, my well-loved teddy bear who sported a camouflage t-shirt with the Maj's picture on the front. Mom had ordered the bear when I was in preschool and the Maj trained at Ft. Riley before he left for Iraq. Tears stained Riley's shirt from the nights that I couldn't sleep because of fear.

"You don't have to be scared." Hoot wrapped her arms around me, and the smell of her shea butter brought back memories of spa nights at our sleepovers. "We know the nights are rough."

"We don't have to sleep." An unruly curl sprang from Bing's head.

"*You* do," we chorused and laughed at our simultaneous response.

"What?" Bing pouted.

"Lack of sleep affects you like a shot of sugar." Mia elbowed her. "Remember last time you stayed up all night?"

We groaned. Bing was like a wind-up toy with a broken spring. The girl chattered until all of our heads spun. She wound up tighter and tighter until nothing would stop—her mouth, her legs, her arms, even her bouncy red curls. The blur of motion finally crashed so hard, we almost called the paramedics because Bing didn't appear to be breathing.

"Anyone up for a game of midnight basketball before we tuck Sleeping Beauty to bed?"

Bing stuck out her tongue, but Teegan was already out the door. "Last one on the court makes breakfast tomorrow."

"Biscuits and gravy sound good." Hoot raced past Teegan and ran for the garage. Saturday morning breakfast with the girls was an oink fest that would make Jellybean jealous.

"I vote for waffles with a mountain of whipped cream and extra strawberries." Bing dove in front of me, motivated by the promise of sugar. If it wasn't for Mia lagging behind, I'd be last on the court.

In no time, the basketball thudded against the concrete. The cold only fueled us. Mia didn't appear for a full five minutes after the rest of us.

"Congratulations." Bing slapped her back. "You're making breakfast."

"Whatever." Mia pulled her coat tighter. "Waffles are easy in the toaster."

43

Something was bothering Mia, but Teegan diverted our attention with the first shot. Basketball was serious. Mia would have to wait.

Without Bronwyn to even the teams, we had to sub players.

"I'll sit out," Mia volunteered too quickly. A cut-throat game of rock-paper-scissors usually decided the teams.

"You sure?" Teegan asked.

Mia took a seat on the porch steps and only nodded. If I wasn't so competitive, I would've called a time out.

Hoot and I teamed up against Teegan and Bing.

"To ten?" Hoot dribbled the ball between her legs without effort. All our time on the court paid off.

Teegan charged, so Hoot passed the ball to me, and I scored a lay-up.

"Nice." Hoot high-fived me, and a dog treat slipped from her pocket. The girl always carried a stash for the animals at the shelter or any other strays she might meet.

Bing grabbed the rebound and zigzagged past us. I flailed my arms in defense, but she ducked and scored.

"Two up." I bounced the ball. When Teegan lunged for me, I switched hands and spun around. The Maj's dog tags jingled under my shirt.

"Fancy footwork." Her lip curled in a combination of disgust and praise.

I arched my hand and released the ball. Swish. The sound was music to my ears. "Thanks."

We battled back and forth between us, neither side distancing the other in points. Mia disappeared inside toward the end of the first game, so we played another round while we waited for her return. Then we had to play a third game to break the tie.

Cold air puffed from my mouth, but I hardly noticed the temperature. Hoot and I were down by two points when Teegan snatched the ball from me. I resisted the urge to spew out profanity.

"Watch and learn." She positioned herself for the perfect jump shot and scored. "We win."

Teegan and Bing body bounced while Hoot and I muttered our congratulations. Revenge was left for the next game. Long ago, we'd vowed to keep the game on the court, not in our friendship.

"I need a gallon of water." Teegan headed inside, and the three of us followed. I'd been so caught up in the competition, I'd totally forgotten about Mia.

"Mia?" I called out in a voice not much louder than a whisper so as not to wake her parents or her younger twin brothers. No one answered.

A light above the stove illuminated the dark kitchen. We'd been in Mia's house enough to know where the glasses were kept, but we avoided the ice dispenser to keep down the noise.

"Do you think she's sick?" I kept my voice low. "Maybe she went to bed."

Bing started to raid the pantry, but Hoot tossed her an apple instead. "It's past midnight. No sugar for you."

She took a big bite and tiptoed behind me toward Mia's room where we found her watching an old romantic movie from her collection.

"You feeling okay?" Teegan brushed her hand against Mia's forehead. "You don't feel feverish. Why'd you skip out on our game?"

"Ignore, Ms. Sensitivity." Hoot sat on the edge of Mia's bed. "Everything okay?"

45

Mia shut off her iPad and exhaled. The light glinted off the diamond stud in her nose. "You ever just want to do something different in high school?"

"Like make the varsity basketball team?" Teegan piped up. Her dad coached the high school girls' team, and she dreamed of being a standout—even as a freshman.

Hoot screeched before Mia could explain. "Look." She showed us the screen on her phone. "Collin's husky had her puppies."

Four pups snuggled against their tired mom.

"Can I have one?" Bing begged. "Please, please, please. My dad's moving out of his apartment to a bigger place next week."

"I'll have to ask. Collin already promised one to Jackson." Hoot didn't talk much about her older brother who'd just completed rehab. His drug use had been tough on the whole family. "Look at that sweet little face." She scrolled to a close-up of one of the puppies.

The others didn't notice Mia wander out of the room, so I followed her to the kitchen.

"Hey, what's wrong?" I hopped onto the counter, and she offered me a bag of chips.

"I want to try out for the color guard."

I tried not to show my surprise. Mia's problems normally involved boys.

"Those are the flag girls who perform with the marching band, right?" I took a handful of Doritos.

Mia nodded.

"That's great." I chomped on a chip. "You'll be a natural."

She lit up. "You think so?" Mia's confidence rarely wavered.

"Definitely. You have the agility of a gymnast and you're strong, so you'll be able to catch the rifles."

Mia bit her lip. "Try-outs are next month. If I make it, my summer will be crammed with practices."

"So why are you worried?" I licked my orange fingers. "Basketball is a winter sport."

She winced. "Because I'm not trying out for basketball in high school."

"Oh." My eyebrows lifted.

"If I make color guard, I want to do winter guard, too."

A sliver of disappointment lodged into my heart. Basketball wouldn't be the same without Mia. She brought flare to the court.

"Promise you won't tell Teegan?"

I crossed my fingers.

"At least till try-outs are over." Mia sighed, again showing a rare glimpse of her vulnerability. "I might not even make color guard."

"You will." I hopped off the counter and gave her a hug. I wouldn't let my disappointment get in the way of my friend's dreams. I just hoped Teegan would feel the same way. I couldn't bear the thought of the girls breaking apart. Life without the Maj was torture enough.

Losing my friends would kill me.

***

Petey was snoring on the couch when Mia's mom dropped me off before taking the twins to their cousins' house. After Mia's favorite uncle died from cancer last year, her large extended family got even

47

closer. Sometimes I wished my family wasn't so spread out across the country, especially with the Maj gone.

"Hey, sleepyhead." I tossed my sleeping bag on the floor and poked Petey.

He buried his head under his paw.

"Lazybones." I laughed.

A note from Mom waited on the counter. She had to work a 12-hour shift at the hospital, so she wanted me to make vegetable stew in the crock pot.

I nuked some pizza rolls and downed a glass of chocolate milk before dicing the carrots and potatoes.

Petey lumbered into the room, so I let him outside. The familiar thump of a basketball could be heard on the neighborhood court.

"Nice shot," I called out to Teegan from our back door. The cold temps didn't deter her. Rain or shine, cold or hot, the girl was a diehard.

She cradled the ball, and the tassel on her stocking hat bobbed. "Want to play?"

"Give me ten minutes."

I'd just finished the stew when my phone buzzed. Condensation made my fingers slick, so the screen didn't respond to my touch.

I hurried to wipe my hands against my pants. The number was from the base switchboard which meant the Maj was on the other end.

"Don't hang up," I pleaded, swiping my finger against the touch screen again. I unlocked the screen just in time to hear the dial tone buzz in my ear. I was too late. A few seconds later, the voicemail chirped.

"Hey, Rooster." The Maj's voice sounded in my ear, bringing a hundred memories. "Just wanted to say 'hi.' Give your mom a hug. I know she's working. I'll call back next chance I get."

"No," I begged the screen. "Please call back. Please."

Angry tears burned my eyes. How could I miss a call when I held the phone in my hand? Why wouldn't the stupid screen work? I felt like I was drowning in an inch of water.

My heart sank as the minutes ticked by without another call. Discouragement numbed my sense of time. I replayed the voicemail, and Petey looked around, confused.

"The Maj isn't here, boy," I choked out through my tears. I couldn't push out the haunting fear that I would never hear his voice again. The tears wouldn't stop.

The doorbell finally broke my trance, but I didn't move. The door wasn't locked, so Teegan twisted the knob and called out my name in a shaky voice. I didn't answer.

She walked into the kitchen and froze, basketball on her hip.

"Rooster, what happened?" Her voice rose at the sight of the tear tracks running down my face.

I clasped the Maj's dog tags in one fist, unable to speak.

"Are you okay? Did something happen to the Maj?"

Fresh tears sprang to my eyes. I raked my free hand through my hair and pulled at the roots like a crazy person. Twelve months on this roller coaster of fear would torture me. I felt like I was losing my mind. "I missed his call."

Her face dropped. "I'm so sorry."

Teegan dropped the basketball, and it thudded against the floor until stopping to rest against the dishwasher. She knelt beside me and wrapped me in her embrace while Petey snuggled between us, his fur tickling my nose.

Teegan didn't say a word until my sobs subsided. I could've kissed her for that kindness. My heart ached, and she didn't try to force happiness.

"He's safe," she whispered when I finally quieted. "Try to focus on that."

I could only nod.

Teegan smoothed the wild strands of hair until I regained my composure.

"A year is too long." I sighed, releasing the dog tags. "I can't do this."

"Not by yourself." She pulled me to my feet. "That's why you have friends. We're here for each other."

My attempt at a smile was pathetic.

"Come on." Teegan handed me a box of tissue. "A game of one-on-one is just what you need."

She grabbed the ball while I blew my nose.

I just wanted to be alone, but Teegan refused to let me hole up in my room. She dragged me toward the door, not even stopping to let me change out of my combat boots. "Start sweating, and you'll feel a hundred percent better."

Complaining was useless. The cold weather wasn't even an excuse. Teegan had a way of making me smile even when I didn't feel like it. A little trash talk unarmed my sadness and pulled me into a friendly competition.

Teegan chucked the ball to me. "Loser buys Gatorade."

"And a candy bar." I dribbled the ball, thinking of a Snickers bar from the Kwik Shop up the street.

"You're on." Teegan guarded me, but I spun around her and made a jump shot. "Two-zero."

She grabbed the rebound. "Only because I went easy on you."

"Whatever," I grunted.

Teegan bolted for a lay-up.

"Lucky basket." I yanked the ball and dribbled down court, netting a perfect long shot. The sound of the swoosh made me smile.

Playing basketball worked its familiar magic. Soon I was in the zone where sweat and competition blended in a perfect combination. My blues disappeared as I pounded the pavement.

Teegan matched my every basket, and our 10-point game turned into all-out war for the most points.

"Water break," Teegan finally rasped after 30 minutes. She dabbed a towel across her forehead.

I didn't argue. My heart thumped against my chest.

We gulped until our bottles were dry, and my stomach grumbled.

"Ready for that candy bar?"

She didn't have to ask twice, especially since we were tied. "Great game."

We bumped fists, and Teegan threw a sweaty arm over my shoulder. "Feel better?"

I grinned as we headed toward the convenience store. A giant Gatorade called my name. The Maj was right. There were miracles everywhere you looked. Basketball. Sweat. Junk food. A friend.

***

"Where have you been?" Mom met me at the door, arms crossed. "I've been texting you for an hour."

"My phone died." I showed her the dark screen as proof. "I was at Teegan's. Sorry. I lost track of time."

"I was too hungry to wait," she snapped. "Some conversation would've been nice."

She and I both knew how little we talked at meals without the Maj.

"Sorry," I muttered. "I already ate."

I should've stopped at the apology. My words sparked her anger.

"Of course you did." Her eyes narrowed. She hadn't changed out of her hospital scrubs. "Why think about anyone other than yourself?"

Somewhere in the back of my head, I heard the Maj's warning not to fight with my mother, but anger overtook reason. The resulting scream fest made Petey bury his head under his big paws.

I finally had to leave before I did something I really regretted.

"Don't walk away from me," she called out.

I clomped up the stairs in my combat boots, planting every step with loud defiance. The slam of my door underscored my anger. I dove under the jungle netting and punched my pillow. A lone feather drifted from a seam under the camouflage pillowcase. If only the Maj were here to intervene, but he was fighting his own war.

Riley looked at me with his glass eyes.

"What?" I voiced out loud to my stuffed friend. "Why did the Maj make me promise to be nice? I can't survive a year with the woman who gave birth to me."

I swear the bear gave me a look.

"The Maj is on a whole different continent," I tried to reason. "He doesn't have to deal with her every stinking day."

I shook my head to clear it. How could any sane person be holding a conversation with a stuffed animal?

Your mom's hurting as much as you, even if you don't want to admit it.

Ugh. I wanted to scream. Losing an argument with my mom was bad enough. Losing an argument with a teddy bear was embarrassing.

Don't push her away.

I wanted to launch Riley through the air, but I stuck in my headphones instead. Mom would nag me about the volume, but I didn't care. So what if the music was too loud. I needed to drown out the crazy voice inside my head. Otherwise I'd spend the Maj's deployment locked up in a mental institution.

***

The clock beside my bed read two in the morning when I realized I'd fallen asleep. Petey's regular breathing was missing. No wonder I'd awoken. My Great Dane's mammoth body usually took up half my queen-sized bed.

I inched open my door and let out a low whistle, but Petey didn't respond. When he didn't come a second time, I crept down the stairs to investigate.

Light from the reading lamp spilled over my mom asleep in the recliner. She clutched one of the

Maj's Army jackets like a blanket. Petey guarded her from his spot near her feet.

"Come on, boy," I whispered. "I didn't let you out earlier."

The tags on his collar jingled, making my mom's eyelids flutter open.

"Sorry." I forgot how light she slept during the Maj's deployments. "Petey needs to go out."

Mom blinked as if reorienting herself. When her gaze fell on me, she cleared her throat. "I'm sorry about earlier, Teegan. I lost a patient today."

I gulped. The Maj knew just what to say when Mom had a rough day at the hospital.

"He was Colter's age. He lost control on an icy patch on the road."

I exhaled slowly, imagining all the worries that must have played through her head when I didn't answer my phone.

"Can I have a hug?" Mom stood, squeezing the Maj's jacket in case I refused.

But even I couldn't be that cold. No matter how mad I'd been. We needed each other.

Coffee and disinfectant lingered on her hospital scrubs.

"I love you," she spoke into my hair.

Petey leaned against us. "Me, too."

I could almost feel the Maj smiling at his girls.

***

The wind found the hole in Bronwyn's jacket and bit her skin. Flurries of snow swirled around her head, chasing another icy blast. Would winter ever end?

"Not much longer." Mama rubbed her arms and eyed the line which snaked around the building. The drop in

54

temperatures drove more people to the shelter. The news predicted record lows for the late March night.

Bronwyn didn't want to scare Kenzie, so she pushed down an involuntary shudder. Too many bodies competed for the available beds. They stood too far back in line, even though Mama made sure they'd arrived early. Seasoned homeless people had arrived long before they'd stepped into line.

What would happen when the beds were all full and there was no more floor space for another mat? Where could they sleep?

Red stung Kenzie's cheeks as if she'd been slapped. The little girl should be watching cartoons like other kids her age. Not waiting in line outside a homeless shelter.

"You okay?" Bronwyn nudged Kenzie. The crowd was strangely quiet, the various bodies numbed by the cold.

She nodded. Her sister never complained.

Bronwyn shuffled forward with the others like an animal being herded into a corral. Humiliation stripped away her self-respect. Strays at the animal shelter had more dignity.

"I'm sorry," Ms. Carmen's voice reached her ears as they neared the entrance. "We don't have any more room." A collective groan rose from the crowd. Panic seized Bronwyn.

"We have a temporary shelter set up at a church two blocks from here," Ms. Carmen hurried to add. She took the red scarf from around her neck and wrapped the wool around a woman without a jacket.

Bronwyn didn't know whether to feel relief or disappointment. She dreaded the thought of walking in the cold after waiting so long. But the alternative was worse. They wouldn't survive a night in these temperatures.

Mama couldn't hide the defeat written on her face. "Come on, girls." She wiped her eyes and straightened her shoulders. "Let's get out of the cold."

Kenzie shivered, but said nothing.

If only they could drive, but the beat-up Corolla that had transported them across the country finally gave out. They'd been forced to abandon the vehicle in a convenience store parking lot. The loss still devastated Bronwyn. They were trapped if her father came after them again.

Bronwyn caught Ms. Carmen's eye as they waited to cross the intersection.

"I'm really sorry." She approached. "Come to my office tomorrow, and we'll get you into Hope's House."

"Hope's House?" Mama narrowed her eyes.

"For women and children," Ms. Carmen explained. "The shelter and soup kitchen are only two components of the mission. Hope's House is a little more permanent than the shelter."

Mama hesitated. "I don't want a paper trail."

"You're cold." Ms. Carmen squeezed Mama's hand. "Let's talk tomorrow."

A horn blared, blasting Bronwyn's focus back on the road. Her stomach grumbled, and brittle toes made walking painful as they crossed the street. She'd give anything for a thick pair of warm socks or a steaming cup of hot cocoa.

Kenzie clutched Abigail to her body, and a snowflake landed on her plastic smile. The favorite doll had been a gift from her preschool teacher.

Streetlights blinked on as they trudged toward the church. A line of people straggled behind them. Bronwyn wiggled her fingers to keep the blood flowing. Even with gloves, frostbite was a threat.

Mama stopped in front of a century-old church sandwiched between skyscrapers. A spire pierced the darkening sky. Muted light shone through a stained glass window.

Bronwyn stomped her tennis shoes outside the building before entering. She hoped the place wasn't drafty. The church could be their home for days. The weather reports predicted the cold spell would linger into the following week.

Bronwyn hated life on the streets.

Chapter Five
April 2012

I threw off my camouflage blanket before my alarm clock rang. If I hurried, I could find the next geocache before Teegan's mom dropped us off at school.

Thirty painfully slow days had finally passed, and I could search for the second set of coordinates. I sprinted downstairs with Petey on my heels and lifted the lid on the foot locker. It had been so tempting to race through the clues. But I'd resisted the urge and honored the Maj's monthly timeline.

My fingers trembled as I flipped through the stack of envelopes and landed on the one designated for April. The paper sliced my flesh, staining the envelope with a drop of blood next to the word "dare." I sucked my finger and read the clue before plugging in the coordinates on the GPS.

"The place I will miss the most."

I sat back on my knees and repeated the words as Petey wiggled his way under my hand. I petted his head while I concluded the obvious. The Maj would miss home the most. Had he hidden the next cache in our house?

The GPS proved my hunch, so I wandered from room to room until I stepped into the kitchen. Of course the clue would be in the room we most frequented. I scanned the countertops and lifted everything from the toaster to the crock pot, but found nothing. The clock on the microwave reminded me of the time. I still had a shower to take before school.

"Five more minutes," I muttered to myself, opening cabinets at random. The clue could be anywhere. My eyes landed on the table, so I dropped to the ground. Nothing. I checked underneath the Maj's chair, and my fingertips touched paper. I pulled off another envelope taped to the underside and tore off the seal, careful not to destroy the contents.

"I dare you to combat your own loneliness by reaching out to a loner. Challenge #2: Sit with someone at lunch who eats alone. Miss you, kiddo."

I gulped down the lump blocking my airway. Crazy how the Maj knew exactly how I felt despite our distance.

Even my friends couldn't completely erase the loneliness that shadowed my days. The Maj's absence weighted my heart.

I folded the challenge and knew just the person.

They called her Jell-O after she got sick in elementary school and puked all over the cafeteria. Red Jell-O was on the menu.

She was a loner. Invisible most days unless targeted.

***

"So let me get this straight." Mia added gloss to her lips and checked the result in her locker mirror before the tardy bell rang. "You basically want to tilt the balance of the universe and switch tables at lunch?"

I nodded. "It's not like we have assigned seating."

"Is this another one of Coach's challenges?" Bing chomped on her gum, referring to our volunteer work with Campus Kitchen last semester.

"Kind of." I kept my answer vague, still not wanting to reveal the Maj's challenges.

Teegan narrowed her eyes, but didn't ask the question on her lips.

"I'm in." Hoot straightened the fliers in her hand. She and Collin were passing out information about an adoption day at the animal shelter. "What's her name again?"

The question made us each pause. None of us knew anything more than Jell-O's nickname. The girl had been in at least one or two of my classes, but I'd never bothered to get to know her. Guilt wagged a finger at me. How could I be so callous?

We agreed to meet at the cafeteria entrance at the start of lunch. Hopefully we didn't scare Jell-O when the five of us descended on her table.

"See you later," Teegan called out to me when the bell broke up our group.

I headed to English, hoping we didn't have to journal today. My emotions were all over the place since the Maj left, and I really didn't want to lose it in class.

Three hours later—and mercifully a break from journaling in English—the girls and I carried our trays across the cafeteria toward a table with a lone occupant. Shaggy hair hung over Jell-O's glasses. She slumped over her lunch, body turned inward like she wanted to disappear.

"Can we sit here?" My voice squeaked like a chewy dog toy.

When she didn't answer, the girls and I exchanged a look. Mia was never completely sold on my idea, and now her body language shouted. *I told you this was a bad idea.*

"Can we sit here?" I repeated the request louder.

Jell-O moved her tray but didn't make eye contact. I couldn't blame her. People were mean to her. I might not pick on her, but I didn't defend her either. I was just as guilty as her bullies.

Teegan and Hoot swung their legs over the cafeteria seat while the rest of us took the opposite side. Jell-O closed a book in her lap and gripped the edge of the table as if bracing herself.

I wanted to tell her we wouldn't hurt her, but words didn't prove much. She probably thought we were luring her in for the kill.

"What're you reading?" I asked instead.

Jell-O ran her fingers along the title before pushing the cover toward me. It was one of my favorites.

"You like *The Lord of the Rings*, too?"

She nodded.

"I'm Josie," I said. "But my friends call me Rooster."

She gave me a funny look at my nickname.

"Something the Maj—my dad—came up with when I was little."

Again, Jell-O gave me a quizzical look, but didn't ask questions.

I pointed to each of the girls and introduced them. "Meet Mia, Bing, Hoot, and Teegan."

"Jada," she muttered so quietly, I almost didn't hear.

"Mind if we eat?" Teegan dug into her hamburger. "I woke up too late for breakfast."

Jada hadn't touched her food. No wonder she was so petite. The girl had the slim frame of a runner.

"Not hungry?" Bing waved a fry in the air before plucking it into her mouth.

Before Jada could answer, Grace and Symone, two of the populars, walked by the table. Last year they made a fool out of Jada when they filled her locker with boxes of Jell-O.

"When did you start sitting here, Mia?" Disapproval shone in Grace's eyes.

Mia looked like she could get sick.

"You okay?" Symone wrinkled her nose. "You don't want to miss the big day tomorrow."

The Barbie clones left before I could send them sprawling across the cafeteria floor. If color guard meant being friends with these two, I hoped Mia bombed the try-outs.

"What's tomorrow?" Teegan piped up.

"Did this drop out of your book?" Mia changed the subject. She handed a photograph with worn edges to Jada.

She cradled the paper, tracing her fingers over the photograph.

"Who's that?" Curiosity spurred Bing past any guilt at invading Jada's privacy.

Unshed tears glossed Jada's eyes. "My brother."

I leaned closer. The kid in the picture could have passed as Jada's twin. He had the same thin face and long nose. Instead of shaggy hair, though, his hair was buzzed, and he was dressed in a military uniform.

"He looks so young," I observed.

A far-off look came over Jada. "He was."

The past tense made my forehead wrinkle. Awkward silence filled the air.

"Jason died last year."

The name jolted me. *Jason Caulier.* The young soldier with PTSD who committed suicide. *Jada was his sister?*

My temples throbbed, making me feel dizzy. The Maj got the call on our way home from a club basketball game. They found Jason in his barracks, a rope around his neck. The newspaper obituary left out that detail, but I heard my parents' whispers.

Post-Traumatic Stress Disorder—PTSD—was a silent enemy. Just as real and ugly as roadside bombs and terrorists, PTSD tormented soldiers long after they left the battlefield. Normal life was impossible. Too many veterans like Jason lost the war inside their minds. Traumatic memories haunted their sleep and shadowed their days.

"I'm sorry." Hoot wrapped her arm around Jada with tenderness. She stiffened at the embrace. No one ever reached out to the girl called Jell-O.

"Me, too," I managed a whisper. My fingers instinctively went to my dog tags.

Bing paled. The haunted look on her face reminded me of the day she told us the news of her parents' divorce.

The bell cut off further conversation, so Jada tucked her brother's picture inside her book. Her food remained untouched.

"Want me to get a pass so you can finish eating?"

She shook her head. "I'm not hungry."

I knew the feeling. Food lost its appeal when fear and sadness lodged inside the soul.

"See you tomorrow?" Hoot asked.

Jada's eyes widened. "Really?"

She looked from me to the girls, and we all nodded. Even Mia, though reluctantly.

It was the least we could do.

***

63

"Is Jada's brother in your dad's unit?" Teegan swung her backpack over her shoulder as we headed outside. No basketball practice meant we walked home.

I shook my head. "He's—was—in the Army."

We exchanged a look at the past tense.

"The Maj was the casualty assistance officer for Jason's family."

"Translation?" Teegan needed my help decoding military acronyms and terms as much as I needed her assistance using sign language with her sister.

"My dad helped with Jason's funeral arrangements and death benefits."

"Whoa." Teegan whistled. "That stinks."

"Someone has to do it." I exhaled, trying to force down my own fears. Every time the doorbell rang, I froze. My knees buckled at the thought of someone walking up our driveway with the awful news that the Maj wasn't coming back.

Teegan and I walked in silence, each lost in thought. Had Jason's mom collapsed into her husband's arms at the news? Had Jada been the one to answer the door?

Teegan finally shook her head. "Poor girl. I had no idea."

"I know," I admitted. "The Maj doesn't talk much about that part of his job, so I didn't connect the dots."

"I feel so bad." Teegan lowered her head. "Jada was in my homeroom last year, but I never even talked to her. She got bullied all the time, and I never said a word."

We crossed the street at the corner and passed the apartments where Bronwyn used to live.

"There's so much we don't know about people, huh?" I thought about how little we'd known about Bronwyn when she joined our basketball team last season. None of us girls had a clue that Bronwyn and her sister went to bed hungry most nights. What more didn't we know about Jada?

We turned onto our street. "Want to work on homework at my house?"

I smiled, grateful I didn't have to be alone in an empty house. Mom wouldn't be home for another two or three hours.

We stopped at the kitchen first, and Teegan pulled out two glasses. "Root beer float?"

If it was basketball season, she'd be grabbing everything from Tabasco sauce to red pepper flakes and jalapenos for our spicy milkshake concoction that served as our good luck charm on the court.

Teegan's dachshund padded into the room while she scooped ice cream into two mugs.

"Hey, Sadie." I patted her head then grabbed the root beer from the pantry. The liquid bubbled into a frothy brown cloud when I poured it over the ice cream.

"Yum." Savanah signed when she burst through the garage door and saw the floats. "Can I have one?"

Teegan scooped ice cream into a third mug, and Savanah laughed when the fizz tickled her nose.

"No burping." Teegan winked, and her sister giggled.

The two were in obvious cahoots. Savanah slurped her root beer and assumed the position— chin tilted down and airway open. The explosion of noise hit the sound waves as soon as her mother walked in the door.

"Savanah Noel Miller." She set down a bag of groceries on the counter and raised her eyebrows at her youngest daughter.

I bit my lip, trying to hold in the laughter. For someone who couldn't hear, Savanah had a killer belch. I wondered if she felt the vibration in her throat.

"Nice." Teegan bumped fists with her sister.

"Don't encourage her," their mother scolded. "I'm trying to raise a couple of young ladies."

"What?" Teegan feigned innocence while holding up nine fingers behind her back. She turned so Savanah could see her score.

The two were a regular comedy act.

Savanah ignored her mother as she went for a perfect score. This time, her burp hit the Richter scale.

"Ten!" Teegan held up her fingers, and Savanah jumped off her stool for a victory dance.

"Show's over." Their mom scooted Savanah toward the garage. "Help Teegan unload the rest of the groceries."

Groans replaced the laughter.

I followed them into the garage and grabbed a bag, remembering the burping wars between my brother and me. My mom didn't appreciate the finer nuances of a great burp either, but the Maj encouraged our contests with his own rip-roaring renditions. Colt even Skyped me on his way to boot camp, and we had the mother of all belching contests over the air.

Thoughts of Colt in his uniform reminded me of Jada's brother. Had she and Jason been close? Did she miss the little things like burping contests and arguing over who got the last Oreo in the package?

66

I had the girls when things got rough, but Jada was a loner at school. Add that to her grief and getting bullied, and the girl must be dying inside. There had to be something I could do, but what?

"Someone's deep in thought." Teegan nudged me as we set down the last of the groceries. "Everything okay?"

"Can I borrow your laptop?"

"Lots of homework?"

I shook my head. "I have a question for the Maj."

Teegan handed me her laptop. "Say 'hi' from me."

I punched in her password and smiled as a picture of the girls filled the screen. Hoot convinced us to participate in an adventure race to raise money for the animal society. Her mom snapped the picture as we crossed the finish line, arms slung over one another, mud covering us from head to toe, and grins spread across each face.

The girls were always there for me. Who did Jada have?

Maj,

I get so annoyed when people say stupid stuff to me. Like my algebra teacher today.

"At least you can email your dad," he said. "It's not like the old days where you have to wait for weeks or months for a letter. You can Skype or Facetime, and it's like you're in the same room."

I wanted to smack him. How does that change anything? You're still not here. And

I'm not there. A hundred emails don't change the fact that you're gone.

But I kept silent. As much as I want to hate my algebra teacher, most people don't know what to say or do.

I feel the same way about this girl at school. Kids call her Jell-O, but her real name is Jada. She was the loner I sat with at school after I found your second challenge.

Remember Jason Caulier? The soldier who killed himself? Remember telling his family the awful news? Jada is his younger sister.

I feel so helpless. Empty words only bring more pain, and I don't want to say anything stupid like my algebra teacher. Is there anything I can say or do?

Signing off,
Rooster

***

Mom's tears stopped me cold when I stepped into the house after hanging out with Teegan all afternoon. She sat in the living room still dressed in her nurse's scrubs.

I clutched the dog tags. Had my worse fear come true?

I dared to look at the entryway. But no one stood in the shadows. No visit by an officer in uniform. No chaplain bearing bad news.

The Maj was okay.

For now.

I collapsed on the couch across from Mom. We could breathe. Another day to cross off the calendar.

My heart hurt at thoughts of the alternative. News of the Maj's death would break me.

"What's wrong?" My voice squeaked.

She held up the television remote in her hand. A commercial played without sound.

I unwrapped her fingers from the controls and turned off the television. "You can't watch the news, remember?"

She wiped a tear and nodded.

News headlines kept us up with nightmares. During the Maj's first two deployments, we vowed to avoid news sources. This round would be no different.

"Come on." I pulled her into the kitchen. "Supper's ready."

I scooped brown rice onto two plates and topped it with vegetable curry.

Mom filled a tea kettle with water for hot tea. We took a seat, but the Maj's empty chair mocked our attempt at ordinary life. I was still getting used to Colter being gone.

"Let's eat in the living room."

I pushed back my chair too abruptly, and it clattered against the wood floor. The noise echoed through the silence.

"How was work?" I attempted small talk as we transferred the food to the coffee table, but it fell pathetically short. Mom could only divulge so much about her patients with privacy laws, and I didn't want to talk about the geocache hunt.

The silence magnified our fears.

"How about Netflix?" Mom suggested, though I could tell her heart wasn't in it. We never watched

69

shows during family mealtimes, but our new normal came with new rules.

Images flashed across the screen, but I couldn't engage in the storyline. My appetite wasn't any better. Maybe Colter could talk if I called him. "Can I be excused?"

Mom looked at me with a blank expression.

Don't leave her.

I stopped mid-stride. I could almost hear the Maj's deep baritone voice fill my head. If Riley was making another telepathic appearance, I needed serious help. My bear friend was stuffed.

She needs you.

I hit the remote, and the screen went blank. Mom didn't even move. She hid these moments from me as a kid, or maybe I was too young to see her fear during the other deployments.

I grabbed a deck of cards. "How about a game of Speed?"

She didn't answer, so I shuffled the cards. "Ready?"

Mom blinked. "What're we playing?"

"Speed." I jumped up to retrieve a bag of Hershey's miniatures. "Winner gets chocolate."

Mom frowned. "You know I don't do sugar."

"I don't plan to lose."

A faint smile crossed her face. I pulled out a box of rice cakes from the pantry and tossed it on the coffee table.

"Your exciting prize."

She smacked me in the arm.

"Would you rather have tofu?" I dealt the cards, and a snort escaped.

"You sound like Colt." Mom grinned now. My brother was famous for his snort fests, but I had yet to uncover my secret talent.

I giggled, and more snorts followed. I sounded like a regular pig. Jellybean would be happy.

Mom leaned back against the couch and gripped her sides.

We spent the next two hours playing cards and laughing. The Maj would've been proud.

***

My heart leapt at the site of the familiar writing on the envelope inside the mailbox the next day after school. The Maj's first letter had finally arrived.

I hurried inside and spilled the contents onto the table. Getting mail from the Maj felt like my birthday and Christmas all rolled into one.

Hi Rooster!

Two months down. I cross off another day when I hit the sack each night.

Staying busy keeps me sane. Otherwise I'd go crazy missing you, Colter and Mom. My days are filled with missions, lifting weights, running, reading, watching old movies, and connecting with the soldiers.

I work inside a qalat, an earthen fortress located within the perimeter of the FOB. We sleep in shipping containers which have been converted to multiple rooms. Not exactly the Hilton, but it's better than a tent.

71

The cooks take good care of us. The chow hall beats MREs any day.

Remember camping in the back country and you begged me to bring a couple packs of meals ready to eat? Most soldiers complain about the shelf-stable food, but you actually had fun heating them up.

So were you surprised to find the second cache inside the house? I knew you'd accept the challenge. Good for you.

I remember Jada from the funeral. A sweet girl, but fragile. She could use a friend like you. That's probably the best thing you can do—be a friend.

April Fool's Day turned into a week-long prank fest with my soldiers. Someone penny locked the door to my room, so I had to climb out of the window. It wouldn't open because of all the pennies stuck in the door frame.

I retaliated with an obnoxious alarm clock I found at the marketplace. Hiding the clock under some bunks made for great entertainment. One guy almost hit the ceiling, he jumped so high.

Apparently they didn't appreciate the wake-up call because I found a goat with a nasty disposition in my room this morning. Yes, an ornery goat named Diablo. He's one of the animals on the small farm we have inside the FOB. Trying to herd him back into his pen made for quite the entertainment. I think half the unit showed up to see me wrestle Diablo. So, now comes my revenge. Any ideas from the home front?

Are you being nice to your Mom?

Love, Dad

***

"My name's Weather." The girl with the short dark hair took a seat next to Bronwyn at breakfast. She wore a pair of baggy brown coveralls that draped her small frame. "What's yours?"

Bronwyn didn't want to make friends. Not here. Not at the mission. The girl stuttered over her words, no doubt high on something. What kind of name was Weather? Bronwyn hunched over her plate, hoping the girl would get the hint.

But Weather wasn't deterred. "Names define a person, you know?" She stammered again, but her words struck Bronwyn. There was a simple wisdom somewhere beneath the dirt and grime. The girl wasn't high; she had a speech problem.

"My name's Mackenzie Nicole Keller," Bronwyn's sister piped up before Bronwyn could answer. "Kenzie for short."

"Don't talk with your mouth full." Mama scolded from across the table. She insisted on manners, refusing to let circumstances rob their dignity. Napkin in your lap. Elbows off the table. Slow, small bites.

"A pretty name for a pretty girl." Weather tucked a stray lock behind an elfish ear. Her simple innocence reminded Bronwyn of a boy she once knew with autism.

"Grams said I was as unpredictable as my name," Weather stuttered as she cut her pancake with a plastic fork. "She called me whimsical. A free spirit."

Something pulled Bronwyn to Weather. Like storm clouds converging on a dark sky. "So, why Weather? Were you born during a blizzard or something?"

"Blue skies." Weather unzipped a pocket on her coveralls and pulled out a frayed picture. She stared at the image for a long time, fingering the edges with nails caked in dirt.

"Can I see?" Kenzie stuck out her hand.

"Finish your breakfast." Mama tried to divert Kenzie's inquisitiveness, but Weather didn't pick up on the nonverbal clues. She pushed the picture across the table and stumbled over her words. "My mom died from an infection a week after my birth."

Bronwyn studied the grainy photograph. The woman had the same brooding eyes and perfect brows as Weather. Short dark hair framed a pixie face.

"She's lovely," Mama told Weather. "You have the same natural beauty."

Weather hesitated, not sure how to accept the compliment.

"Does your grandmother live around here?" Bronwyn handed back the picture.

Weather shook her head. "Grams died last year. From cancer. I've been on the streets ever since."

Bronwyn bit her lip. She couldn't imagine being alone on the streets without Kenzie and Mama. "How old are you?"

"Seventeen next week." Weather leaned close enough that Bronwyn could smell the syrup on her breath. "You going to eat that?"

"Take it." Bronwyn pushed her sausage link toward the edge of the plate. "I have to get to class."

Weather stabbed the sausage. "I get hungry eating for two."

Bronwyn swallowed her shock. Weather was pregnant?

Weather rubbed her stomach, and Bronwyn could see the small bump under the baggy coveralls.

74

"Her name's gonna be Lily." Weather's voice got husky with emotion. "Like a flower."

Mama squeezed Weather's hand. "Do you have help? Are you seeing a doctor?"

Weather took another bite. "I don't like doctors. They didn't save my mom or Grams."

"I'm sorry." Compassion brimmed Mama's eyes. "Maybe I could take you to a clinic."

Weather stared at her food, so Mama didn't press the issue. "Can we can talk later? We have a bus to catch."

Weather swirled the syrup with her fork and didn't answer.

"Maybe your baby will go to my school when she's big like me." Kenzie adjusted the straps on her Hello Kitty backpack.

"Someday." Longing pooled in Weather's eyes. "School was tough for me."

Bronwyn gulped. The familiar dread of returning to a new school paled when she considered the alternative. Life could be worse. Had Weather dropped out of school after her grandmother died?

Kenzie picked up her plate and waved. "See you later."

Bronwyn couldn't help but stare at the ragtag bunch in the room as she headed for the trash. An old man with shifty eyes talked to himself in the corner while two women in a heated conversation spouted profanity without any regard for the volunteers serving them.

Weather sat alone on the bench they'd deserted, her petite frame even more exaggerated from a distance. She wasn't much older than Bronwyn. A shelter hardly seemed like the place for such a young girl.

How could Weather raise a baby living on the streets?

Chapter Six

I did a double take when I walked into Coach's seventh period geography classroom with Mia and Teegan. Someone who resembled our teacher stood near the windows wearing frayed jeans and several layers of dingy clothes. Holey shoes covered her feet while unkempt hair spilled from a worn ball cap.

"Is that Coach?" I asked the girls under my breath. She showed up in everything from native clothing to period costumes, but this latest getup was odd even for Coach.

"I think so." Teegan narrowed her eyes.

"That's Coach, alright." Mia craned her neck. "Unless she has a twin who needs a serious wardrobe makeover."

"Nice outfit, Coach," Hoot's boyfriend, Collin, called out behind us. "What're we doing today?"

Coach's unconventional teaching methods still surprised me. Somehow she kept her job even when we wrestled sumo-style while studying Japan or ran through the halls in a mock Running of the Bulls for our unit on Spain. The last two weeks of school promised more adventure.

"What's that smell?" A student named Jace darted into the room seconds before the tardy bell rang.

Coach walked down the aisle between Mia and me, and my eyes watered from the stench. She smelled worse than our locker room after practice. "I haven't showered for a week."

"Want to use some of my perfume?" Mia didn't hide her disgust, but I didn't react. When the Maj and I camped in the back country, we didn't shower for several days.

"No thanks." Coach's eyes looked bloodshot from lack of sleep. "Any guesses why I'm dressed like this?"

"Your washing machine broke?"

"You want to conserve water?"

Coach smiled at the chuckles. "Actually I spent the weekend on the streets. I wanted to blend in so I could get more from my experience."

Her answer brought momentary silence.

"Homelessness is the theme of our year-end project." She leaned against her desk. "What comes to mind when you think about homelessness?"

"Bums and drunks," Jace blurted out.

"People pushing grocery carts," Collin added.

"Veterans," Teegan answered, and I knew she was thinking about old Larry. Bing's former neighbor lived in a house with a pot-bellied pig until his death, but he could've easily landed on the streets with his PTSD. We thought the guy was nuts until we met him and learned his story.

"What about kids your age?" Coach walked toward the white board. "Have you ever considered the faces behind homelessness?"

Teegan and I exchanged a look.

"Bronwyn," she mouthed, and a sick feeling washed over me. Where did Bronwyn and her sister sleep at night?

"Homelessness is a complex issue." Coach uncapped a marker and wrote down a web address. "Teens are often the most invisible and vulnerable. Some statistics say age nine is the average age of homelessness."

Several of us gasped.

"Check out the Homeless Challenge Project online tonight for your homework assignment. Browse some of the journal entries from the participants and then read my thoughts which I've posted on our class page."

I jotted down the website. Investigative reporting always intrigued me.

Teegan raised her hand. "Are we going to sleep on the streets?"

Coach shook her head. "As much as I'd like you to participate in the Homeless Challenge Project, sending 150 middle school kids for a couple nights on the streets is a big risk—even for me."

"What if we get permission from our parents?" Collin asked. He and Hoot were always on a crusade to save the animals. This project would only fuel his social activism.

"The liability is too great." Coach scanned our faces. "But there's an alternative. If your parents agree, you can join me and a few chaperones for a night in Cardboard City."

Once again, Coach had our attention. Her uncanny ability to pique our curiosity made learning fun. Several hands shot up in the air.

"I know you have lots of questions." Coach handed out a form. "But I'm not going to give you specifics. If you're interested, ask your parents to sign the permission slip and show up at school this Friday night. Dress in layers and leave all electronics at home." She looked across the room, mystery glinting from her eyes. "And bring your own cardboard box."

The bell rang as Coach called out the last of her instructions. "Read through the handout tonight. Tomorrow we'll be in research mode."

Teegan and I waited for Mia to zip up her binder which bulged with homework. Not many people got past her looks to know the girl who couldn't decide which she wanted to pursue more—cosmetology, fashion design, or law school.

"So, you girls in?"

I flashed a double thumbs up. If this project was anything like working with Campus Kitchen, I knew I would never look at homelessness the same.

Mia slung her backpack over her shoulder and headed out the door. "How can we say no?"

***

I microwaved a bag of popcorn and plopped on the couch with my laptop. The website Coach recommended suggested sticking with a partner for the homeless challenge. The project came with risks, so safety was top priority. The site also popped my investigative idea, stressing that the homeless challenge project wasn't some undercover mission or journalism exposé. Homeless people weren't animals at a zoo to be watched. They were real people.

Several participants commented on their experience, including one whose observation made me recoil in horror. Homeless people slept on cardboard away from food if they didn't want to wake up to rats crawling over them. I shuddered in disgust. Beady eyes and furry claws filled my mind as other words jumped off the page.

Rejected.

Ignored.

Invisible.

How would I feel after Friday night's experiment? I logged onto our class webpage, and Coach's blog drew me like a good book.

6:01 p.m. Friday night.

I left school after the last bell to come to the city after learning about the Homeless Challenge Project. Homelessness is an issue even in our community, but I didn't want to risk running into people I knew.

Two hours later, I am standing on a street corner with a cardboard sign. The friend I'd invited canceled last minute, so I'm all alone.

"Hungry. Please help."

Tattered rags replace my normal teaching and coaching clothes. Unscented baby oil makes my hair look even dirtier than two days without a shower.

Plastic jabs the bottom of my foot. My driver's license and medical insurance card are buried inside my sock.

Shame makes it hard to look at the drivers who pass by me. Most talk on their phones until the light changes, hardly aware of my presence. I push a strand of oily hair behind my ear.

I might as well be invisible.

8:06 p.m.

I pass a movie theater and the buttery smell of popcorn makes my mouth water. A couple walks out of the building, hand in hand. He tosses a half-empty bag into the trash, and for a brief moment, I think about dumpster diving, but I remember the caution on the website about discarded needles. I've only been on the streets a couple hours, and already I feel less human.

10:32 p.m.

Fear heightens my awareness. Every sound sets me on edge. The blaring of a car horn. The hiss of a radiator. The low rumble of a distant train.

I long for my own bed. The safety of my own home. I feel so vulnerable out in the open. The four walls of my bedroom are replaced by the vast expanse of sky. My stomach growls. I didn't eat anything for supper. Begging at the street corner only brought scorn. I've never been so utterly humiliated in my life. Not embarrassed humiliated. Self-worth humiliated.

I don't want to take a bed at the shelter from someone who really needs it, so now I have to face the night alone. I'm so tired, but I don't dare fall asleep.

1:23 a.m.

I huddle under a street lamp, grateful I can return to my home after my experiment. This hope alone helps me stay strong. What about the many who have no hope?

7:32 a.m.

My head pounds from lack of caffeine. I need a strong cup of coffee and a couple aspirin. My back is stiff from sitting on the concrete. I pass the shelter, and I am surprised to see one of my former students leave its door. He doesn't recognize me, and I'm too shocked to say anything. My heart sinks. I knew his home life was rough, but I never expected to see him on the streets.

10:35 a.m.

I have to go to the bathroom, so I step into a convenience store. The clerk gives me a death look and tells me I have to buy something. I walk out, trying to hold in the tears. The golden arches beckon me from across the street. I take the side door and avoid eye contact. The smell of food assaults me. I'd give anything for a cup of black coffee and a sausage biscuit, but I don't have any money. I hurry to the restroom before someone chases me outside.

I almost don't recognize myself in the mirror. The eyes that stare back look haunted. My experiment has made me painfully aware of my own vulnerability. What separates me from people on the street? Good health, a job, a supportive family. A string of unfortunate circumstances, and everything could change. My hands tremble at the realization. I stick them under the warm stream of water, and dirt swirls down the drain. A lady waits behind me. I can feel her eyes. I hurry to leave.

2:03 p.m.

I jolt up to a rock pelting my shoulder. Laughter pinpoints the culprits. Two boys on skateboards circle my park bench, targeting me. Even the day brings little rest.

"What's the matter?" the one with the skunk hair sneers. "Park bench too uncomfortable? Maybe you should try upgrading to a door stoop."

His friend howls. "Five star accommodations, for sure."

I square my shoulders. I may be at my lowest, but I refuse to stoop to their level.

A rock skids to a stop at my feet. I vow my students will never be so callous.

5:17 p.m.

Boredom makes the day drag to a crawl. I want to sleep, but my last run-in makes me leery. I wander aimlessly up and down the streets. Strains from a guitar pull me toward a street corner where a young man strums the strings. His story plays out in the chords, but few listen. The sun glints off a handful of quarters in his case. He might have enough for a sandwich from a deli. I lean against a brick wall and let the music carry me away.

7:18 p.m.

A woman stuffs a couple dollars in my hand, and I stutter in surprise. I've had nothing to eat for 24 hours. I try to mutter my thanks, but I'm too choked up to talk. I buy a hotdog at an outdoor stand and devour it in seconds.

I'm tempted to give up my experiment, but I don't want to quit. Not when my goal was two days on the street.

I dread another night out in the open, so I find an all-night diner. I count the leftover change in my pocket, hoping it's enough for a cheap cup of joe. Nothing fancy from a coffee shop tonight.

An hour later, the manager asks me to leave. I've overstayed my welcome. Worse, the sky is overcast, and I don't have a plastic sheet to keep me dry.

I drag myself outside and wander the streets for another night. I want to shower in my own home and sleep in my own bed and open the doors to my refrigerator and eat whatever I want. I'm exhausted, hungry, and miserable. If this wasn't an experiment, I don't think I would survive.

Coach's last words haunted me. I couldn't shake my fear that Bronwyn and Kenzie were on the streets. What could I do? I had no idea where they were. I felt so helpless.

***

Mama smoothed out the pleats in the grey skirt and eyed her image in the foggy mirror. The thrift store smelled like mothballs and cast-offs, but Mama was excited about the outfit she'd found. After Ms. Carmen connected them to the women and children's shelter at Hope's House, she helped

Mama work on her résumé and get an interview with the school district.

"How do I look?" She bit her lip.

"Amazing." Bronwyn looked up from the book she'd found for a dime. "Like you're going to impress the principal and get the summer teacher's aide job at Kenzie's school."

Her sister played with a grungy teddy bear she'd found in a bin of stuffed animals. "Theodore says you look beautiful."

Mama was too nervous to smile at Kenzie's imaginative play. "Is it too noticeable?" She untucked the white dress shirt and pointed out a stain.

Bronwyn shook her head. "The skirt will hide it."

Mama touched her bare collarbone and frowned. "This neckline is too plain."

She disappeared into the fitting room, so Bronwyn took Kenzie to look at the jewelry encased under glass at the front of the store. Mama had sold the last of her jewelry long ago.

"Can I look at that necklace?" Bronwyn pointed to a silver chain with a heart pendant. The clerk unlocked the case and handed her the necklace.

"It's so pretty." Kenzie's eyes lit up. Like many little girls, she would be decked out in hair bows and matching accessories if they could afford the luxury.

Bronwyn turned over the tag, and her eyes bulged. Mama would have to go without the necklace.

"We have some cheaper costume jewelry over there." The clerk pointed to a bin of plastic jewelry.

Bronwyn tried not to hide her disappointment. Mama wasn't playing dress-up. She had a job interview.

Bronwyn returned the necklace and trudged back toward the fitting room. Mama could make sweats look like they came off a modeling runway. But still, professional clothes accented with jewelry would help her chances.

If only Mama could get her feet in the door as a teacher's aide during summer school, just maybe she could teach again.

When Teegan, Mia, and I showed up at the school Friday night with our cardboard boxes, I had a strange sense of déjà vu from volunteering in Coach's class last semester. Instead of the college cafeteria kitchen, however, we were outside our school. Temporary barricades blocked off a huge section of the parking lot. Several of our classmates milled about the enclosure along with adults wearing lanyards. Cardboard boxes lined the perimeter.

"Nice outfits," Mia teased Teegan and me. She was famous for turning her Goodwill finds into masterpieces. We just looked like bums. "You could've at least washed your hair."

Teegan ignored Mia's sarcasm and scanned the crowd looking for the college-aged leaders we'd volunteered under when we prepared and delivered food for Campus Kitchen. "I keep thinking Nick and Annie will show up."

Mia had a crush on Nick until she learned he and Annie were engaged. Now she was more focused on the smart phone she had to give up for the next 24 hours.

Coach appeared at the makeshift entry having showered and changed clothes. "Electronics can go here." She stuck out a container which held a half dozen iPods and phones.

"Told you to keep it at home."

Mia stuck out her tongue at Teegan, and I stifled my laughter. I fished my phone out of my pocket and handed it to Coach. I hoped I wouldn't miss a call from the Maj.

"Start with that station there." Coach pointed to a table manned by two volunteers. "They will give you an ID and your assignment."

We had to drag Mia away from her phone before the withdrawals hit. It wasn't above her to kiss the bling-encrusted case.

"Welcome to Cardboard City, girls." The guy on the right smiled. He found our IDs while the other volunteer explained what we needed to accomplish.

"You have three assignments before you leave here tomorrow." She gave us an index card. "They are listed here if you forget."

I skimmed over the three tasks. 1. Find a safe place to sleep. 2. Eat three meals. 3. Gain income of some kind.

"How?" Teegan asked, but the volunteers wouldn't answer.

According to the ID attached to my lanyard, I was a teen runaway who'd been on the streets for three weeks. Apparently my home-life was so abusive, I preferred the streets. Teegan was a chronic homeless man with mental health issues.

I wanted to tease her about being a nutcase, but Mia's description hit too close to home. She was a veteran who had spent two tours in Iraq and suffered from a brain injury. The description could've matched several of the soldiers in the Maj's unit, making me wonder if any of them had been homeless.

"Where do we start?" Teegan asked, but the volunteers broke us up.

"Forget who you were. You are now the individual described on your ID." The guy pointed to our lanyards. "None of your descriptions suggest you'd be friends on the street."

I waved goodbye to the girls. I already didn't like our little experiment.

A volunteer passed me. A lanyard around his neck read "police." I turned in the opposite direction, figuring if I was a teen runaway, the last person I'd want to visit would be a police officer—even if he could help me.

I didn't want to carry my cardboard box around all night, so I found a place to set it up. My stomach grumbled. Coach had told us not to eat supper, and now my insides protested.

A line had formed in front of a tent where two people served soup, so I made my way toward the crowd. Collin waved when he saw me. According to his ID, he'd lost his job six months earlier and got evicted from his apartment when he couldn't afford the rent.

Another person in line told us he'd been a cancer survivor, but huge medical bills forced him to the streets.

I swallowed my shock. I'd never considered the reasons behind homelessness, and the descriptions surprised me. Any of these people could be my next door neighbors.

Standing in line for soup felt strange, especially after being on the other side with Campus Kitchen as a volunteer. As I took the bowl of soup, shame and gratitude clashed inside me. This was a mock exercise. I wasn't really homeless; so why did I find it so hard to look at the person serving me?

Since there weren't enough seats, I stood near the barricade, cradling my plastic bowl. One sip of the bland soup made me wish for cornbread and a bowl of beef stew. The Maj made a killer pot of meaty goodness over a campfire.

Someone knocked into me, jarring my daydream and sending my bowl flying. So much for eating. The soup kitchen had already closed for the night. I cursed my rotten luck.

I wandered around the Cardboard City for an hour, passing a pretend bus stop, a make-believe hospital, a fictitious jail, and a makeshift public housing office. Volunteers passed me wearing nametags such as social worker and police, but I didn't stop to talk, afraid they'd send a teenage runaway back to the house of horrors I wanted to escape.

A whistle blew, and Coach asked us to assemble in the gym for a panel discussion. I followed the crowd inside, grateful for a chance to sit. My old shoes pinched at the toe.

There weren't any rules for sitting by our friends, so I scanned the bleachers for Mia and Teegan. I couldn't find Mia, but Teegan caught my eye and waved for me to join her. My stomach grumbled as soon as I took a seat. Being homeless was hard— even if the experiment was only pretend.

"You didn't eat?"

I frowned and told her what happened.

"Sounds like my night." She played with the cord on her lanyard. "I tried to get help at the hospital, but they sent me back to the streets because I didn't pose any danger to myself or others."

I started to ask a question, but Coach wanted our attention. Three others joined her at center court. After Coach thanked us for being willing to get out of our comfort zones, she introduced the panel—

Shanda, Max, and Alison. All three had once been homeless.

Teegan turned to me with wide eyes. "No way."

I couldn't believe it either. Shanda looked like a model, Max reminded me of my grandfather, and Alison could've stepped off a treadmill, she was so fit. Not one of them looked like my mental picture of homelessness.

Shanda told the audience that she'd been kicked out of her house when she got pregnant her senior year of high school. After couch surfing for months, she landed on the streets. The state took away her baby when she tested positive for drugs. She vowed to get her child back, so went to rehab, finished her GED, and worked full-time while going to night classes. Shanda was now a nurse and mother to her three-year-old son and living in an apartment.

Max got laid off from a factory job after 29 years and lost his home when he couldn't make the payments. Temporary jobs didn't pay the bills, so he lived in his truck until he finally managed to land a permanent job as a mail carrier.

Alison looked familiar when she took the microphone, but I couldn't figure out why until she told us about her son. As soon as she mentioned the name Jason, my jaw dropped. I looked at Teegan and saw the blood drain from her face. Alison was Jada's mother.

We listened as Alison told the audience how Jason joined the Army like his dad. He was a great soldier, but after 15 months living in a war zone, Jason came home a different person. Nightmares haunted him day and night until he eventually took his life.

91

No one moved. The silence magnified Alison's tears. When she regained her emotions, she recounted the difficult days ahead. The divorce, the weeks she couldn't muster the strength to get out of bed, the loss of her job, the eviction notice, and life on the streets.

I could barely breathe. *Jada had been homeless?* How many times had I passed her in the hall—clueless that she left school each day to return to the streets?

After two months on the streets, Alison got grief counseling and help. She never revealed Jada's name, but said she and her daughter lived in a mobile home and recently started training for their first half marathon to raise awareness of veterans suffering from PTSD.

My stomach churned. How could I be so blind to kids like Jada and Bronwyn who went to my school and lived in my neighborhood?

After the three shared their stories, Coach opened the panel for questions, and one after another of my classmates came to the microphone.

"What was the hardest thing about being homeless?"

"Where did you spend your nights?"

"What's the best way I can help someone on the streets?"

The questions didn't stop.

As I listened to the panelists, homelessness morphed from this huge social issue to a problem with a face. Single moms. Tired soldiers. Scared teenagers. My heart hurt from their collective pain.

We spent the next hour making personal care bags for the local homeless shelter. An assembly line of bodies filled small bags with a bar of soap, a bottle of shampoo, a razor, a tube of toothpaste, and a toothbrush. I would never waste another trial bottle from a hotel again. Items I took for granted were a lifeline for someone on the streets.

When we finally left the gym, night had fallen, making me shiver, even with the warm temperatures. I didn't even have a blanket.

I reviewed the three tasks on my lanyard and figured trying to earn money would be even harder than getting supper. I headed to my cardboard box.

My perfect spot had been overtaken by a group of my classmates, so I dragged my box to a quieter spot. Trying to get comfortable was impossible without a pillow and a sleeping bag. My extra layers bunched at the knees and elbows, making me feel like an overstuffed marshmallow.

Sleeping in a tent while camping with the Maj was one thing. Sleeping in a cardboard box was a whole different story. The sides closed down on me, making me feel claustrophobic. I couldn't imagine doing this every night.

After tossing and turning for what seemed like forever, I finally gave up and crawled out of my cardboard home. A few adult chaperones wandered the length of the parking lot keeping watch over us. I took a seat on the curb and touched my dog tags, wondering if the Maj was gazing up at the stars, too.

A flashlight bobbed a few feet away, stopping in front of me.

"Hey, Josie." Coach shined the light into her face to identify herself. "You okay?"

"Yeah. I just can't sleep."

She took a seat beside me. "Lots to process, huh?"

I nodded. "Did you know about Jada?"

93

Coach bobbed her head. "Jada wrote about living on the streets in her English journal, so the school social worker got involved. That's how she and her mom got help."

"I never really thought much about homelessness," I confessed. "I thought people on the street were bums and drunks."

"You and me both," Coach admitted. "My parents weren't rich, but we always had food on the table and a roof over our head."

I lifted my lanyard with its description. "I never considered the circumstances behind homelessness. I'm so worried about Bronwyn."

"Me, too." Coach sighed. "I think about her every day."

"Do you think she and Kenzie are on the streets with their mom? Like Alison and Jada were."

Coach's hesitation made my heart sink. "I don't know. I wish I knew."

"That's what so tough." I hugged my knees. "If I only knew where they were, maybe we could help them."

The night settled around us, magnifying the silence. There weren't any easy answers.

***

I woke up with a stiff neck and hunger pangs. My teeth felt grainy, and I wanted a hot shower. Around me, groggy bodies emerged from their cardboard boxes with bed head. I jammed on a ball cap, just imagining what I looked like after my restless night.

Three hours later, my attempts to earn money fell short, but I managed to eat a brown banana and watery oatmeal at the fictitious homeless shelter. Life 101 on the streets was kicking my butt.

Somehow Mia's hair and makeup were perfect like always, but Teegan looked like I felt. Bags lined bloodshot eyes.

"Rough night?"

Her nostrils flared. "Thanks to the streetlight shining in my eyes and the loud snores coming from the cardboard box next to me."

We trudged toward the check-out table. Mia looked like she wanted to dance the tango with her phone. Going unplugged had been her biggest challenge.

A half dozen messages lit up my screen.

"Ohmigosh." I fumbled with the buttons. "I need a ride to the hospital."

"What happened?" Concern filled Teegan's voice.

"One of the soldiers. His wife. Baby." My sentence came out choppy as I skimmed the messages.

Teegan's mom honked at us.

"Text me when you know something," Mia called after us.

"There's been an emergency." Teegan's mom sped away from the school. "A soldier's wife arrived by helicopter this morning."

"Is she okay?" I snapped my seatbelt. Teegan's mom flew down the streets like a NASCAR driver.

"Her water broke." She took a corner too fast. "I guess the baby's not doing good."

My blood chilled. Two soldiers in the Maj's unit had babies on the way. Only one was far enough along to deliver, and even then, the baby would be two months early. Harrison's wife, Katrina.

95

The hospital was 15 miles away, but Teegan's mom made record time. She nearly took out a guy in scrubs when she dropped me off at the emergency room door.

"Sorry," she called out of the window. "We have a baby emergency."

He rushed to help us, and then stopped in confusion when I sped past him. I didn't have time to explain.

"Want me to come inside?" Teegan called out, but I was already through the automatic doors. I'd call them later.

I found my mom in the waiting area. She stood on shaky legs when I rushed toward her. Worry lined her eyes. Her skin was ash white. Being a nurse made her all too aware of every possible outcome—good or bad.

"How's Katrina?"

Surprise filled Mom's face. She hadn't mentioned the soldier's wife's name in the text.

"I met her camping with the Maj," I hurried to explain. "When we went into town to wait out the storm."

"Ms. Jameson?" A nurse called her name. "Katrina asked for you. We're delivering the baby."

"I gotta go." She squeezed my hand. "Call Teegan's mom if you want to go home."

Mom disappeared behind the double doors, but I couldn't leave. I kept thinking of the Maj's promise to watch over Harrison. I felt the same weight for his family.

I flipped through a magazine when a familiar figure rushed toward the front desk, apron strings flying. Grey hair sprung out of the clip holding Grammie's hair at the nape of her neck.

"Katrina Harrison my great grandbaby are they okay?" She didn't take a breath.

"I'm sorry," the nurse said. "But I can't give out that information without consent from the patient."

"Privacy laws?!" Grammie's small frame swelled with rage. "I drove over 100 miles to get here like a bat out of you know where. Katrina's husband is halfway across the world. Defending. Your. Freedom. I'm it for her family. Find a way around your privacy laws. Now."

The nurse backed her chair away from her computer screen. "Uh, let me talk to my supervisor. I'll see what we can do."

Grammie eyed the people in the waiting room, and our gaze met.

"Josie?" Her hazel eyes lit up, and she threw her arms around me. "Is your mama back with my Katrina?"

I wiggled out of her grip and gave her the few details I knew.

"They're delivering the baby?" she stammered. "But Katrina is only seven months along."

"She's in the OR." The nurse appeared. "The doctor is performing an emergency C-section."

Grammie's voice trembled. "I can't go back?"

"I'm so sorry." The nurse shook her head.

Grammie collapsed into my arms, so I guided her back to the chairs. "Mom's with Katrina. She's not alone."

Her voice cracked, so I handed her some tissue. Grammie cried while I held her hand. Veins crisscrossed her skin like little blue rivers. The minutes ticked by on the clock over the television. A home renovation show played on the screen.

A man checked in a kid wearing baseball pants. The boy favored his left arm. Behind them, a guy waited in line holding a blood-soaked towel against his head. A baby screamed from behind a closed door. Could Harrison sense what happened back home even though he was half a world away? Did he know he was about to become a father?

I dozed off until a hand shook me awake.

"Wake up, you two." Mom's voice broke through my fog. Beside me, Grammie straightened in her chair.

"Congratulations." She hugged Grammie. "You have a beautiful great grandson."

"A great grandbaby?"

"Katrina's still asleep after the C-section, but we can see little guy in the NICU."

Worry clouded Grammie's eyes.

"His lungs need to develop more," Mom reassured her. "But all the tests look good. He's a little fighter."

"Like his daddy," Grammie beamed.

We took the elevators to the second floor. A nurse buzzed us through the NICU doors, and we stood in front of the glass window. Five babies in tiny diapers rested under warm lights in incubator beds. Tubes crisscrossed their small bodies.

"There he is." Mom pointed to the bed on the end. A sign read Baby Harrison. Four pounds. Sixteen inches.

"Look at him." Grammie put her palms to the glass. "He's a little baldy."

I marveled at his tiny features. The smallest nose and lips made up his perfect face. Little legs and arms barely filled the incubator.

Grammie counted ten fingers and ten toes. "Does his daddy know yet?"

Mom shook her head. "Things happened too fast. Katrina should be waking soon. Then she can Skype him. And little guy can get a name."

My stomach grumbled, so we headed to the cafeteria. By the time we finished, Katrina was awake, sitting at the nursery window in a wheelchair. Her blonde hair was tousled, and her skin looked pale against the hospital gown. Her hand touched the glass. Silent tears trickled down her face.

I felt awkward intruding on her pain.

"It's okay, baby." Grammie wrapped her arms around Katrina. "He's healthy. And you're his beautiful mama."

She hung onto Grammie's neck. "I want to hold him so bad, it hurts."

"I know, baby. I know." Grammie smoothed her hair. "It won't be long."

"My husband isn't here, and I can't even kiss my new baby." Katrina sobbed. "No one told me it would be so hard."

Emotion welled inside me. Katrina had to shoulder so much. Fighting the enemy wasn't the only battle in this war.

I swallowed the lump in my throat. Mom knelt in front of the wheelchair. "You are strong."

Katrina lifted her chin.

"You are brave. You can do this."

Katrina bit her trembling lip. "I'm not strong."

Mom smiled through watery eyes. "Look at him." She pointed to the baby. A nurse adjusted one of his tubes. "He needs you to be strong. Your husband needs you to be strong."

Katrina could only nod through her sniffles.

99

"Grammie's here. We're here." She squeezed Katrina's hand. "Just focus on one day at a time."

Grammie's phone chimed. "Someone wants to meet his new son." She handed the phone to Katrina who lit up and wiped her eyes with the sleeve of her gown.

Harrison filled the screen wearing his helmet and camouflage. He cradled a weapon in his hand.

"Congratulations, Daddy." Katrina put on a brave face. "We have a little boy."

Harrison couldn't speak. Tears trailed the camo paint on his face. Katrina gave up trying to hide her own. Emotion overcame each of us.

Mom regained enough control to motion for the NICU nurse. "Could you get a close up of baby? This soldier would like to meet his son."

The nurse took the phone and disappeared behind the glass. She panned the camera across the length of the incubator then returned the phone to Katrina.

"He's so little." Worry cracked Harrison's voice. "Is he going to be okay?"

Katrina nodded. "He just needs a little time." She couldn't hide her pride. "He looks just like you."

Harrison broke down.

I stepped back to give them their privacy. Grammie talked to the nurse while Mom wrapped her arms around me, and I leaned into her embrace.

Katrina's voice drifted toward us. She clutched the phone with a trembling hand that couldn't touch her newborn or her husband. I hurt for her.

"She's stronger than she knows." Mom read my mind. "Things will be rough, but Katrina's gonna be a great mom."

Sometimes I couldn't wait to grow up. Today was not one of those days.

"I remember when I thought diapers and no sleep were hard." Mom laughed. "And now I have a son in the military and a teenage daughter." She looked me in the eye. "I still lose sleep worrying about you both."

Grammie would stay with Katrina for the night, so Mom made plans to return to the hospital the next morning.

"Call me anytime." She squeezed Katrina around the neck. "Even two or three in the morning. I have my phone on the nightstand."

"Thank you," she mouthed while Grammie embraced us both.

Mom turned to me. "Ready to go home?"

I stifled a yawn. My own bed never sounded so good.

***

Mom was gone when Petey and I woke up at noon the next day. Apparently my body was still recovering from my night in the cardboard box. Sleeping on concrete every night would kill a body.

"We have dishwasher and trash duty," I read Petey the note from Mom. "Or, at least I do. Then we'll go on our geocache hunt."

Petey rested his head against the table in resignation. "Don't look so glum." I laughed. "I'll be done with chores in no time."

I ate a Pop-Tart while I put away the dishes then grabbed the trash. Petey padded downstairs behind me and waited while I opened the foot locker. The word "together" was written on the third envelope. I tore open the seal and read the clue under the coordinates. "Countless hours are spent here with friends."

The obvious answer was the basketball court which was empty when I looked out the back window. Perfect. No muggles to observe me. Something told me I would need a ladder, so I headed for the garage. Petey ran ahead of me toward the target.

My theory proved correct on the GPS screen, so I positioned the ladder against the backboard.

"Don't break your neck," Teegan called out, startling me. My knees wobbled, so I jumped down to break my fall.

"Thanks." I frowned, disappointed at being discovered.

"What are you doing?"

Teegan knew me too well to lie. My secret was out.

"Geocaching. The Maj left me one cache for every month he's gone."

Her eyes lit up. "Really? Your dad's so cool."

I climbed back on the ladder.

"So what have you found so far?"

"Challenges." I ran my hand along the smooth surface, careful to check the seam at the edges.

Teegan leaned against the post. "Challenges like what?"

"Like sitting with a loner in the cafeteria rather than focus on my own loneliness."

Understanding hit Teegan. "So that's why you sat with Jada?"

"Uh huh," I muttered, focused on finding the cache. When I didn't find anything unusual, I turned to the brackets connecting the post to the backboard. "Bingo."

I pulled out an empty medicine container tucked into a crevice between the metal and jumped to the ground. My dog tags clinked together.

"So the Maj hid 12 different caches for you to find while he's gone?" Teegan took the container from my hands. "Impressive."

We peered through the clear orange plastic. "What's inside?"

I popped off the top and a folded twenty-dollar bill fell into my palm along with a note.

"Money?" Teegan squeaked. "Lucky."

I pressed out the creases on the paper and read an African proverb, "'If you want to go fast, go alone. If you want to go far, go together.' Challenge #3: Buy a tub of ice cream and enjoy it with your friends. Don't use bowls."

"I'm in." Teegan helped me with the ladder. "So how's the baby? Your mom called with the news."

"Little. He's only four pounds."

Teegan whistled. "How long till he gets to leave the hospital?"

I shrugged. "Hopefully by the time his dad comes home for his two weeks of leave."

"That would be so hard." Teegan's eyes clouded with compassion. "Talk about one happy homecoming."

I could just imagine Harrison picking up his son for the first time. His big hands would dwarf such a small body.

A horn blared. Grammie parked her Cadillac behind Mom.

Teegan and I hurried toward them. "How's Katrina?"

"Resting." Grammie grinned. "Charlie's doing great."

"They named him?"

She pulled out her phone to show us pictures. "Charles is a family name. His daddy's name is actually Charles Adam Harrison, but everyone calls him Adam."

Or Harrison if you were one of the soldiers in the unit. I could just picture a little camouflage onesie with "Harrison Junior" stitched onto the material.

"Can you put fresh towels in the guest room and change the sheets?" Mom headed inside. "Katrina gets to leave the hospital tomorrow."

"With Charlie?"

Mom shook her head. "Not for a couple weeks."

"I'm going to enjoy a cup of coffee with your mom before I head back to the restaurant," Grammie added. "She's been so gracious to offer your home to Katrina while Charlie's in the NICU."

The idea of house guests made me smile.

Teegan headed for her house. "Rain check on that tub of ice cream?"

Grammie raised her eyebrow before following me inside. "Ice cream? Maybe I could stick around for another half hour before I hit the road."

***

The smell of detergent sweetened the air at the laundry mat two blocks from Kenzie's school. Bronwyn folded clothes as her sister sat cross-legged on the counter beside her.

"I hope Mama gets the job." Kenzie clasped her hands. "Then I can go to summer school, too."

What other kid wanted to go to school in the summer? But school meant hot lunches and a safe place to go. Bronwyn

104

ignored her nerves by focusing on the task at hand. She creased the edges on a worn t-shirt and wondered about Mama's interview.

"Maybe the principal will ask easy questions like her favorite color or her best friend's name." Kenzie twisted her mouth in concentration. "Not hard questions like 7+2."

Bronwyn bit her lip so she wouldn't laugh. Too bad life wasn't as simple as basic addition. Mama had been voted "Teacher of the Year" when he snapped. A teacher's aide at Kenzie's school would be a good fit, maybe even a chance at getting a teaching job in the fall.

Bronwyn folded another shirt and brushed her hand against the frayed collar. They might not have many clothes, but Mama insisted they keep clean.

"Help me with the socks." She handed Kenzie a colorful pile. "Mama should be done any minute."

Kenzie grabbed a sock and twisted it around the match while Bronwyn folded another t-shirt. She could imagine Kenzie entertaining Teegan's sister Savanah with sock puppets. The two girls had a rare bond.

A game show blared from a nearby television. The door jingled, and Mama stood silhouetted against the light in the outfit she'd selected at the thrift store. Her grin made Bronwyn's heart soar.

"You got the job?"

Mama nodded. "I start tomorrow." She tweaked Kenzie's nose. "I'll be in the kindergarten and first grade wing with you."

Kenzie squealed in delight, her braids dancing with her movement. "Really?"

Mama hugged her. "I better enjoy this now. When you're Bronwyn's age, you won't want me in your classroom."

Bronwyn smiled. She could imagine worse things. "Congratulations."

"So do we get to move into our own apartment?" Kenzie hopped down from the counter.

Mama picked at her nail polish—another rarity. "It's a temporary job. There are no guarantees for this fall." Her expression was wistful. "But it's a job. And being around kids again will be a treat."

Bronwyn had already done the math. A teacher's aide didn't earn much more than minimum wage. Waitresses made more with tips.

"Can we get ice cream to celebrate?" Kenzie begged.

Mama looked at Bronwyn. "Did you use all the quarters?"

She held out her hand. A single coin rested in her palm. "There's one left." Bronwyn kicked herself for not stuffing more clothes into the machine to save a few more quarters.

Mama put on her game face, the one she used to mask the daily strain. Dark bags underscored her eyes. Bronwyn worried Mama would break under all the pressure.

Kenzie flashed a winning smile. "It's okay, Mama. I'll draw you a picture of a cone with three scoops."

Tears welled in Mama's eyes. "Pay day. I promise."

Chapter Eight

Sweat beaded my hairline and trickled down my forehead. I wiped the perspiration with a corner of my shirt before my eyes stung. After our night in Cardboard City, Teegan, Mia, and I convinced our principal to hold a year-end game between the teachers and the girls' basketball team to raise money for the homeless shelter.

A few months earlier, the same event—along with a generous gift from Bing's neighbor, Larry— had saved Campus Kitchen. Nick and Annie had delivered the surprising news during half-time. I hoped today's game would make a similar difference to the shelter.

"Rooster!" Mia tossed me the ball. I took off for the hoop and scored a lay-up. I kissed my dog tags. Since the game wasn't official, Coach let me wear my chain.

The crowd went wild. We were the favorites, and the bleachers were full. Who wouldn't pay a couple dollars to get out of class early?

A flash of yellow and black caught my eye. Savanah was in the crowd, shaking her pom-poms. Teegan's little sister got out of school early to see her play. She was the game's biggest cheerleader. I smiled, thinking of the day the Maj would be back in the crowd rooting for me.

Seeing our teachers out on the court was always a riot, especially our algebra teacher with his skinny white legs covered in long tube socks. If it weren't for some old school moves and questionable plays, we'd completely dominate the teachers. Coach was the only real threat. She'd taught us all our moves.

Teegan blocked a shot and dribbled toward our basket. I tore off after her, falling into the zone where all other distractions faded, and the ball took center stage.

I made another lay-up. Mia scored three baskets in a row. Hoot rebounded the ball after Bing fouled our English teacher and almost took out the referee. I finished out the half with a long shot. We were ahead by ten.

"Nice offense." Teegan slapped my hand when the buzzer sounded. "We got this."

The girls and I took buckets through the bleachers for loose change during half-time while Teegan took the microphone and made a plea for the homeless shelter. My own bucket got heavy as kids emptied their pockets of pennies and dimes. When we met back on the court for the second half, I looked over to see the teachers huddled around Coach. Knowing her, she had something planned to even out the score.

"Teachers rule," they screamed and broke their huddle.

"What?" I adjusted the waistband on my shorts and caught Coach's eye. "No rap song this time?"

She smirked, but said nothing. We'd teased Coach for hours about the ridiculous rap song the teachers had attempted to pull off during our last fundraiser.

Her silence should've made me nervous, but I linked arms with the girls. Our war cry echoed through the gym. We were ahead. No way would we fall behind during the second half.

A tall guy in blue basketball shorts walked onto the court and joined the teachers. He towered over their motley group.

"Who's that?" Mia's eyes widened, perfect eyebrows arching. If she'd had time to powder her face to accentuate her high cheekbones, she would've made a run for the bathroom. The girl was already drooling.

"The band director's student teacher." Hoot exhaled. "Look. He practically touches the basket."

I'd seen the guy in the hallways at school, but he looked taller out here on the court.

"Meet our secret weapon." Coach winked at us. "Good luck, girls."

I started to protest, but Teegan held me back. "Don't let him intimidate you."

Easier said than done. The guy dwarfed all of us, including Teegan who was the tallest girl in our school.

I had to admire her. She didn't back down at the tip-off. The whistle blew, and the referee tossed up the ball. Secret Weapon Dude didn't even jump. His fingertips stretched above Teegan's head and made contact with the ball. The guy weaved around me before I could even blink. The swish of the net sounded seconds later.

Anger erupted across the crowd. Our fans were not happy.

"Shake it off." Teegan grabbed the ball and dribbled down court. "We still got this."

Secret Weapon Dude was a shot of energy to the teacher's team. He made up the point difference with hardly any effort while sweat dripped off me. We ran back and forth, barely maintaining our edge.

When Mia missed an easy shot, I wanted to scream. Her distraction with Secret Weapon Dude would cost us the game. She practically batted her eyes when he grabbed the rebound and zigzagged around our players to make the shot. I groaned as the teachers evened the score. The game was tied.

Teegan called a time out. Her temple throbbed, showing her irritation. If it weren't for the crowd, Teegan would have it out with Mia.

"Sorry." Mia bent over in our huddle and exhaled. "I shouldn't have missed that basket."

"It happens," Hoot encouraged her. "You'll make it next time."

I clenched my fists, trying to relax. Hoot's peace tactics didn't curb my competitive spirit. I wanted to throw something.

Bing fixed her headband, but it did little to contain her mass of curls. "Their secret weapon's killing us."

Teegan eyed the clock. "Two more minutes. Think we can pull ahead?"

I grunted my doubts.

"We win either way." Hoot lifted her head above the huddle and nodded toward the crowd. "Every person here represents a secret weapon in the war against homelessness."

Hoot was right. When we donated $1,401.38 to the homeless shelter after the game, I knew we'd won. Beating the teachers didn't matter. Beating homelessness was the real battle.

***

Mom was on the phone with Dad, so Katrina rapped lightly on my bedroom door. "Think I can do a load of laundry? I don't have much until Grammie brings me clothes this weekend."

"Sure." I followed her downstairs to show her where to find the laundry soap. While Katrina started her wash, I grabbed an opened package of Oreos from the pantry. "Cookie?"

"Thanks." Katrina took two. "The double stuffed ones are the best."

I poured us milk.

"Oreos are the only store-bought cookie I eat. Grammie spoiled me with her home cooking."

"You two seem close."

Katrina twisted off the top of her cookie and licked the frosting. "She took me in my junior year when my parents got busted for running a meth lab. I was waiting tables, and she gave me a room."

I didn't know what to say, so I mumbled, "Sorry."

"It is what it is." Katrina shrugged. "I'm just glad I have Grammie."

"Do you keep in touch with them?"

"Only because Grammie says I should write once a month." Katrina pursed her lips. "Visiting's too hard."

I couldn't imagine visiting my parents behind bars.

"Grammie started training me to cook last summer." Katrina smiled. "I worry about her, but getting her to slow down is like trying to tame a mustang. Grammie's a stubborn one."

"So did she introduce you to her grandson?"

Katrina shook her head. "Adam was two years ahead of me in school. He came home from basic training, and we hit it off."

I could just imagine the young soldier craving home cooking and falling for the cute waitress at his grandmother's café.

"We were planning a big wedding when he got orders for Afghanistan."

"So you got married at the court house?"

"Crazy, huh?" Katrina twisted the ring on her finger. "I turned 19 the next day."

"So you're just newlyweds?"

"And now new parents." Her eyes widened. "I don't have a clue what to do."

"None of us do." Mom came into the room with wet eyelashes and puffy eyes. "Dad says 'hi,' Rooster. He couldn't talk anymore, so he'll call back later."

I swallowed my disappointment. More than two weeks had passed since I last heard his voice.

"Just about the time you figure out the baby stage, they're teenagers." Mom elbowed me. "Most days I'm on my daughter's bad list."

I made a face and dunked my Oreo into my milk.

Katrina raised her eyebrows. "And you're okay with adding my hormones to the mix?"

Mom poured herself a cup of coffee. "Caffeine makes everything better."

Katrina snorted, giving us all the giggles. I reached for the last Oreo, and Mom yanked the package toward her. "Mine."

I should have given her the cookie. Obviously Mom's emotional state was weak if she wanted sugar. But I couldn't resist the competition. I snagged the Oreo and threw my hands in the air for victory.

The motion threw Mom off balance, and she toppled off the stool onto the floor.

Silence dropped like a bomb.

Katrina and I peered around the island. Mom busted out laughing, and we joined her, howling like three crazy people.

"Stop." Katrina clutched her stomach where she got stitches. "Or I'm going to pee my pants."

"Bathroom's that way." Mom stood and pointed toward the restroom. "I call the one upstairs."

I had to cross my legs. Watching them both waddle off sent me into another fit. It felt so good to laugh.

***

Three weeks passed in a blur with all our visits to see Charlie in the hospital. Getting to finally hold him made my heart swell. I swear Charlie smiled at me, but Mom said he probably just had gas since babies don't smile for several weeks. The night before Katrina got to bring Charlie home, the muffled sound of crying woke me up.

Petey followed me to Colter's room, the room Katrina used when she wasn't at the hospital. Seeing Mom comfort Katrina reminded me of my brother. On nights I was afraid because the Maj was in Iraq, Colter would give up his bed for me and sleep on a beanbag. The sound of his breathing was enough to lull me to sleep.

Light spilled on Katrina's face, illuminating two tracks of tears. A sick feeling made my legs go weak. I steadied myself against the door frame and touched the dog tags. Had something happened to the Maj's unit? "Everything okay?" I squeaked.

Mom motioned for me to join them. "Grammie had a stroke."

113

Relief competed with new fear. The Maj was okay, but what about Grammie. "She's gonna be fine, right?"

Mom shook her head. "One of the regulars found her in the kitchen. Grammie died in route to the hospital."

Blood gelled in my veins. I couldn't move. "But she can't be dead." Images filled my head. Grammie playing cards in the cellar with us during the storm. Grammie laughing at our house just days earlier. Grammie holding her new great grandson for the first time.

"No. I don't believe it," I stuttered. "She's supposed to come tomorrow for Charlie's homecoming."

Katrina's hands shook. She was trying so hard to be strong. With her parents in jail and her husband deployed, she was all alone with a new baby.

Tears welled in my eyes. I didn't know what to say.

"I wish I could talk to Adam." Katrina hugged her torso. "He and Grammie were so close."

Mom pulled her into her embrace.

I felt bad for Katrina. Adam was headed home on leave to see his wife and new baby. Now he'd have to bury his grandmother. The weight would shadow the joy of becoming a new daddy.

"At least he'll be home for the funeral." Katrina straightened her shoulders. "I'm grateful for that."

My gaze fell on a picture of Katrina and her husband resting on the nightstand. Adam stood behind Katrina, arms slung over her in a hug. She grinned from under his Army cap. Next to their picture was a photo of Grammie holding Charlie.

She'd crocheted the blue cap that topped his small head.

I couldn't help but remember the Maj's promise to Grammie. Charlie and Katrina were depending on him to bring home their soldier. Now more than ever, Katrina needed her husband.

***

After finally falling into a fitful sleep, a nightmare made me bolt up in bed. My heart threatened to explode in a panic attack. I flipped on the lamp to chase away the shadows. My clock read a minute past midnight. Sweat beaded my lip.

The Maj wasn't trapped inside a casket beside Grammie. Unmoving and cold to my touch. Eyes unblinking.

I gulped in air. I was having a nightmare.

The. Maj. Wasn't. Dead.

I repeated the words until my breathing slowed. I had to get out of bed to shake the haunting images from my head. My feet touched the cold wood floor. The Maj was safe. He was alive.

The squeak of the floorboards would wake Mom, but I couldn't stay in bed. Fear would consume me.

What if the Maj never came back? What if the next funeral I attended was for my dad? The thought knifed my heart.

I longed to talk to Mom, but I didn't want to wake her. And I didn't want her signing me up for counseling.

Petey brushed up against me as if to remind me I wasn't alone. My hand grazed his head, and he licked my fingers. Wet slobber and his coarse tongue brought a smile to my lips.

"I love you, too." I wrapped my arms around his neck. Petey nuzzled into me, and I inhaled his earthy dogness.

I didn't let go for a long time.

Sometimes I couldn't help but wonder if guardian angels came with fur.

***

Communal living grated on Bronwyn's nerves. Mornings used to be her favorite time of day. The smell of Mama's coffee brewing. The sound of songbirds. The blush of color on the horizon.

But now she hated the very act of opening her eyes. Cold reality shadowed every step. Hope cracked into slivers of dread and despair.

A low sob jarred her.

"Kenzie? What's wrong?"

Tears streaked her sister's face in the bed beside her. "She's gone."

Mama jolted upright. "Who's gone, baby?"

"Abigail," Kenzie moaned. The doll with the painted freckles was nowhere to be seen.

Bronwyn frowned. The doll had been Kenzie's comfort during the days and nights of uncertainty. What would her sister do without her faithful friend?

"Maybe Abigail got cold during the night." Mama searched the covers. "Did she snuggle under your blanket?"

Kenzie hugged her knees and rocked back and forth. "Where could she be?"

116

Bronwyn hated seeing the innocence slip from her sister. How could someone stoop so low as to steal a little girl's doll? She thought about the woman with the cobra tattoo in the next room. Bronwyn didn't trust her or her oldest daughter. The girl had more than anger issues.

"Let's eat breakfast," Mama whispered. Keeping a low profile was key to their survival. "We'll figure something out later."

Bronwyn grabbed her backpack. She kept her hair pulled back and slept in her clothes. The simpler the morning routine, the quicker they could leave for the day. Hope's House was better than the wall-to-wall bunks at the shelter, but avoiding people in the communal bathroom kept the stress to a minimum.

"You hungry?" Bronwyn nudged her sister.

Kenzie wouldn't budge.

"I bet Ms. Jenny made scrambled eggs," she tried to coax her sister. The Filipino lady with the big smile was their favorite volunteer at the soup kitchen. She was always sending them off with a bag of homemade chocolate chip cookies or a sandwich to save for later.

"Abigail's not coming back, is she?" Kenzie hugged her knees tighter.

Mama crawled beside her, and Bronwyn followed. They sandwiched Kenzie between them while she cried.

Neither spoke. Bronwyn held her sister's hand. If only she could make everything better. But there was nothing she could do but hold Kenzie.

Sometimes tears were the only answer.

Chapter Nine
June 2012

The dark cloud of death hovered over our house as Mom and Katrina discussed funeral details. Finding the next geocache was the perfect escape.

I slipped on shorts and a t-shirt and opened the next clue in the garage.

"Many who have gone before leave this earth without facing me." The words confused me, so I plugged in the coordinates. Maybe something would click as I pedaled toward the cache.

Humidity made my shirt stick to my flesh. I passed the neighborhood pool, tempted to join the kids splashing in the water. Maybe the girls could meet here later. Mia had just gotten a new bikini. She couldn't wait to show it off.

The coordinates pointed south, so I turned on the gravel road near the u-pick apple orchard. Lilacs sweetened the air. I was less than a mile away from the cache.

Many who have gone before leave this earth without facing me.

I mulled the clue over in my mind as I crunched along the gravel. A meadowlark sang from a fence post. A spire rose in the distance from an old country church. Headstones dotted the nearby hill.

I almost crashed. My heart thudded in my chest. The next cache was in the cemetery?

Every part of me wanted to turn back. Even though the Maj had no way of predicting Grammie's death when he planned the hunt, the irony was too much.

I stood there arguing with myself until a car passed by on the street. The driver probably thought I was an idiot.

"Fine," I huffed before I realized I'd spoken out loud. I'd go to the cemetery, but the Maj and I were going to have some words later. I mean, seriously, what was he thinking? Anxiety nearly killed me already.

I pushed my pedals as fast as they could go so I didn't have to spend another second in a graveyard. The entrance, a wrought-iron structure with the name of the cemetery welded into the design, gave me the creeps. The place looked forgotten.

The GPS pointed ahead, so I leaned my bike against the fence and sidestepped a row of granite headstones. The church had been built in the early 1900s, so the dates fanned back through time. A small headstone marked the grave of an infant.

I walked past a faded plastic flower arrangement and thought about Katrina. She would probably wear a thin path next to Grammie's grave with as much as she would visit.

Loving mother. Hard-working father. Brave soldier. I read the headstones, wondering what Grammie's would say.

How did you summarize a lifetime in one or two phrases? Did it all boil down to the date of our birth and the date of our death? What about the stuff that happened during the dash?

Teegan would snap me out of my philosophical ramblings. But what else could I do? I was stuck alone in an empty cemetery.

Jameson. The name jumped off the headstone, making my flesh prickle. I stared at my last name.

Who was Erwin Jameson? A long lost relative?

119

Light reflected off something hidden in a clump of grass at the base of the stone, so I knelt to the ground. My fingers connected with a small plastic container. The lid popped open with little effort. I spilled the contents into my hand—a note and a small photograph of the Maj and me on a back country hiking trip.

I exhaled, and the puff of air lifted a stray piece of hair. I left the house to escape death, not confront it.

"I know you worry about me, Rooster," the Maj wrote. "But don't let death rob you of living. The reality is I might not come home. But a hundred other things can cut a life short. Cancer. A car accident. Armed robbery. Challenge #4: Don't let yourself die inside. Live every day like it's your last."

I flipped over the note. "P.S. We're not related to Erwin Jameson."

My knees cracked when I stood. The Maj was right. Obsessing over death didn't help anything, but it was still hard not to worry.

I tucked the container into my pocket and retraced my steps to my bike. When I was little, the Maj chased away the monsters under my bed with his imaginary monster ray gun. He'd drop to his knees and blast the underside of my bed until the monsters evaporated.

I pedaled for home. Too bad the Maj didn't leave me a ray gun for my worries. Somedays the fear loomed larger than a horde of monsters. I couldn't imagine life without my dad.

***

"Do I look fat in this dress?" Katrina smoothed her hand over her stomach when I got home from the cemetery. She was a mess of nerves. Harrison was scheduled to arrive at the airport sometime after supper.

"You just had a baby." Mom hugged her shoulders. "Your body will be back in no time."

"But Adam . . ."

"Adam will think you're beautiful," Mom finished her thought. "He won't be able to keep his hands off you or his son."

I buttoned the strap on Charlie's denim overalls. Mom and I couldn't resist buying them to celebrate his homecoming. Charlie had gained enough weight for the doctor to release him from the NICU, but his tiny body still drowned in the preemie outfit.

"You get to meet your daddy today." I buckled Charlie into his car seat. "He's gonna be proud of his little fighter."

A lump lodged in my throat when I thought about Grammie. She would be beaming with pride.

"I don't know why I'm so nervous." Katrina hugged Mom and then me. I tried not to choke on her extra perfume. She was worse than Mia.

"It's normal," Mom reassured her. "Adam will be just as nervous."

"You sure you don't want to come to the airport?" Katrina invited us.

Thankfully, Mom declined. I couldn't bring myself to go. Seeing Harrison in his camouflage would be too hard. The Maj wouldn't take his leave until all his soldiers first had the chance.

We walked out to the little Honda Accord, and Katrina laughed. "Probably won't be long till we trade this in for a minivan. Adam wants a platoon of little soldiers."

We exchanged another round of hugs before Katrina got into the car.

"Wait." I ran inside to grab a huge stuffed giraffe I got for Charlie. Even though we'd see him at the funeral, I was going to miss having the little guy around. Our house would be too quiet again with just Mom and me.

"He's adorable." Katrina looked from the stuffed animal to the small interior of the Accord. "And big."

She squeezed the giraffe into the back next to Charlie's car seat. "Perfect."

I linked arms with Mom. Watching the giraffe's head bob out of sight provided comic relief. A good thing. Otherwise the two of us would've been standing in a puddle of tears. Adam was gonna fall in love with Charlie.

***

"How are my girls?" The Maj's face froze on the screen with his mouth distorted and his eyelids half closed. The pose would normally make me laugh, except the longing to see him made me desperate. I was still reeling from seeing Grammie's lifeless body inside the casket. I never wanted to go to another funeral in my life.

"Come on," Mom muttered at the bad connection. We were huddled around the laptop in our pajamas, Saturday morning cinnamon rolls forgotten.

I held my breath. This was the third time this morning we'd tried to Skype without success. The wireless connection was too sketchy.

My gaze fell on the pictures resting on our fireplace mantle. A photo of the four of us, skin and hair powdered in red, white, and blue after a 5K for Army families was the Maj's favorite. He'd packed a copy of the same photo when he left for Afghanistan. Beside the family picture was an ornate silver frame of the Maj and Mom dressed up for a military ball. I could trace the shoulder cord on the Maj's dress blue uniform in my sleep. His eyes twinkled, like he'd just told the photographer a joke. Peace replaced the worry lines on Mom's face.

Unlike now.

She ran a hand through her freshly brushed hair and frowned. Her skin paled against the lipstick she'd applied.

The screen went dark.

Mom tightened the knot on her bathrobe and dumped her half-eaten breakfast in the trash. She disappeared upstairs without a word.

Disappointment lodged in my throat. I didn't even get to wish the Maj a Happy Father's Day before the screen froze.

Deployment sucked.

***

Bronwyn didn't want to open her eyes because that meant pulling herself from the dream, the one where she and Mama and Kenzie lived in a home of their own. Nana had told her enough stories of her girlhood home that she could picture the little painted house in the country where she longed to live.

Yellow shutters.

Flowerboxes on every window.
Climbing roses on a white trellis.
Wildflowers in the surrounding fields.
A litter of kittens.
A roan-colored horse named Sunset.
A piglet named Juniper.

The dream was so real Bronwyn could even feel a shaft of sunshine warming her head as she lay against the cool floorboards in the hayloft.

Mama's shadow fell over her. *"Wake up, sleepy head."*

Bronwyn's eyes fluttered open, and the little painted house vanished, dissipating into hundreds of shards of broken light.

"I'm headed to work." Mama stood next to the bed. Kenzie grinned, her fingers hooked on the straps of her backpack. She loved having Mama in her classroom. *"Ms. Carmen's expecting you in the kitchen."*

Bronwyn swung her legs over the side of the bed and hugged her sister.

"Love you." Mama kissed Bronwyn's forehead. *"See you this afternoon."*

Fifteen minutes later, Bronwyn snapped on a pair of gloves and stood next to Ms. Jenny in the food line. She could barely understand the woman's broken English, but there was no mistaking her big heart. The Filipino lady talked to everyone and had a hug for the dirtiest person, no matter how much they reeked.

The woman with the cobra tattoo came through the breakfast line with her daughters. Bronwyn avoided eye contact. She wasn't in the mood for a conflict.

"You play music today?" Ms. Jenny scooped eggs onto the oldest girl's tray.

Her voice softened, surprising Bronwyn. *"Only if you come listen."*

"I be there." Ms. Jenny clapped her gloved hands. "You play flute like angel."

Bronwyn stole a quick glance at the girl as she handed her a piece of toast. Dark eyeliner ringed brown eyes, but a rare smile played across her face. Maybe Bronwyn had misjudged her. Maybe she hadn't stolen Abigail.

Ms. Jenny nudged Bronwyn after the girl left. "She play on corner downtown. She famous someday."

No wonder the girl was always so angry. Playing on a street corner to survive couldn't be easy.

Ms. Jenny knew something about everyone who came through the line. An old veteran loved war history. A young boy had a rock collection. A woman with a lisp enjoyed doing crafts.

"Happy birthday." Ms. Jenny produced a cupcake for a lanky man with a scar running down his cheek. She lit a candle and broke out in a solo. The guy looked like he could cry.

Ms. Carmen came by after cleanup and announced the arrival of a dozen kids from a church youth group. They would be packing brown bag lunches to serve over the weekend. Bronwyn's breath caught. A kid from her school stepped into the room. If only she could become invisible.

"We go to school together, don't we?" He lit up.

Bronwyn suppressed her groan. So much for hoping he didn't recognize her.

"Are you volunteering over the summer, too?"

"Yeah," Bronwyn stuttered, sure her face betrayed her secret. She flashed back to the awkward moment Teegan stood in front of the door to her apartment with a box of donated food.

125

"Did you two have any classes together?" Ms. Carmen interrupted their conversation.

"I'm not that lucky." He adjusted his glasses, but it didn't help. The lopsided angle matched his crooked grin.

Bronwyn felt a warm rush of blood. He was cute in a science lab coat sort of way with his pensive blue-grey eyes and tousled hair.

"I'm Oliver, by the way." He stuck out a wiry arm and shook her hand.

"Bronwyn." She was grateful when Ms. Carmen handed out gloves and gave instructions.

"Thanks for coming today." She smiled at the kids who towered over her slight frame. "More hands mean less work."

Ms. Carmen organized them into an assembly line to streamline the work.

"Any pointers?" Oliver flanked Bronwyn's side. He was painfully close, making her fidget.

"You want bread duty?" She handed Oliver a loaf then unwrapped a slice of cheese. Another girl added meat while one of the leaders folded the sandwich in plastic. The rest of the line added carrots, chips and a cookie to the brown bag.

Oliver made small talk while they worked. Bronwyn avoided details about herself, but found out he lived on a lake and had two German shepherds. Mia would tell her not to be so cautious, but Bronwyn couldn't let down her wall.

"Do you like to jet ski?"

Bronwyn admitted she'd never tried.

"Then it's a date." Oliver grabbed another piece of bread. "You have to come hang out at the lake sometime."

Bronwyn gave an evasive answer, but Oliver didn't notice. He was too excited telling her about his family's boat.

The pile of bags grew. Oliver's fingers brushed up against hers as he handed off the last slice of bread. The shock of pleasure made Bronwyn bite her lip. She didn't want to open her heart.

What would Oliver think if he found out she was homeless?

Chapter Ten
July 2012

The smell of chocolate curled under my door, tempting me to shake my sour mood.

"I made cupcakes." Mom knocked.

"Go away." I clutched my dog tags. I'd rather pout than pretend to be happy. I didn't want to celebrate my fifteenth birthday without the Maj.

"Why don't you get dressed?" Mom pushed something under the door frame. "Your friends will be here in an hour."

Curiosity got the better of me. I emerged from under the jungle netting and caught my reflection in the mirror. Static wreaked havoc with my hair. Riley would be keeled over laughing if the bear really did speak.

The envelope proved to be July's geocache. The word "regret" made me wonder what I'd find, especially since nothing had arrived from Afghanistan No birthday package. No special delivery. Nothing.

I pulled the index card from its envelope. "Happy birthday, Rooster. Find this month's cache in a place commemorating your first year. Your gift is waiting there as well."

Was Mom in on the secret, too?

My pity party was over. I had a cache to find.

I headed downstairs, reflecting on the possibilities. My baby book? A family photo album? Video footage from our home movies?

I struck out with the baby book but hit the jackpot with the family photos. The GPS pointed me to the living room where a stack of photo albums rested on the bottom shelf. Most of our pictures were digital files on the computer, but Mom printed some of her favorites to display in a handful of albums.

Early pictures of my parents' wedding and their years before kids filled the first album.

"What're you laughing at in there?" Mom walked into the room wearing an apron.

"Look at your hair." I pointed to a picture of her and the Maj on their first anniversary.

"Big hair was the rave." Mom grinned. "I went through a can of hairspray to get it that high."

She took a seat beside me on the couch, our knees touching as we flipped through more pictures, stopping when memories brought a story.

"Look at you two." Mom brushed her fingers against a picture of five-year-old Colter holding me in the hospital. My tiny fist grasped his finger. Even then, it was obvious I looked up to my brother.

A piece of paper poked from behind the next picture of me asleep on the Maj's chest as he snored in the hospital chair.

"What's that?" Mom's eyes glinted with mystery as I pulled the note from the sleeve.

I'd found the cache. "You knew about this?"

She gave a playful shrug. "Maybe. What does it say?"

I unfolded the note and read the Maj's familiar writing. "My biggest regret is missing out on all the moments of your life while I'm away. I wish I could be there for your birthday, Josie."

Mom sniffled.

"Your birthday gift from me this year is a trip together when I get back. You get to choose where we go. Challenge #5: Live life with no regrets."

"Really?" I searched Mom's eyes.

She nodded. "Wherever you want to go."

I didn't know what to say. A dozen ideas filled my mind, places the Maj and I dreamed about when we were out camping or geocaching. Backpacking in the Rockies, snorkeling in the ocean, hiking down the Grand Canyon. How could I choose? For once I was glad I still had time before the Maj returned so I could think about what I wanted to do.

"Happy birthday." Mom stood and kissed the top of my head. "Ready to frost some cupcakes?"

I leaned back on the couch, both stunned and excited. I started to close the photo album when a picture caught my eye. I must've been five or six judging by my pigtails and missing teeth. The Maj and I rocked together in a hammock, our heads touching and our gaze fixed on the clouds above. I could almost hear his voice as he filled my mind with places to visit. Even when I was a little girl, he'd encouraged me to dream.

"Thanks, Maj," I whispered. "No regrets."

***

Bing was the first in the wave pool at the water park a few hours later. She came up sputtering, red hair streaming into her eyes.

"Come on." Teegan pulled a tube out into the waves. "Bing can't have all the fun. It's summer vacation."

I splashed into the water with Hoot on my heels. Mia sat on her towel in her new bikini, absorbing the

130

rays. We'd be lucky if she joined us on the lazy river. She'd be surrounded by a group of guys in no time.

I dove under water and surfaced near the tube. Droplets beaded my dog tags. The waves made it hard to get on top of the tube, but I finally succeeded only to have the waves stop.

"Seriously?" I groaned.

"We can do the slides and come back when the waves start again." Bing pointed to the side-by-side slides that towered over the park. "First one to the top gets shotgun on the ride home."

Last time I'd been on the insane 15-story slides had been a race with the Maj. The extreme wedgie was worth beating him to the bottom.

Hoot shook her head. "Count me out. I don't do heights and fast together. I'll hang with Mia."

Teegan and I hustled after Bing. She swerved between people to beat us to the top of the slides.

"You won." I caught my breath and slapped Bing's hand. A sickly green color replaced her rosy cheeks.

"I don't feel so good." Bing's knees wobbled.

Teegan steadied her. "Don't even think about hurling."

"Let's take the chicken exit." I pulled Bing out of line before a rain of puke hit the foot traffic below.

Bing didn't answer. She couldn't stop staring at the ground.

"Come on." Teegan pried Bing's fingers off the rail. "Truth is, the slides scare me, too."

We sandwiched Bing between us and slowly made our descent. Bing kissed the ground as soon as we hit the last step.

"Someone feels better." I couldn't help but laugh at her butt stuck up in the air. Nothing kept Bing down for long.

We found Mia talking with Symone and Grace when we returned. Bikinis showed off their perfect tans.

"Hey, guys," Mia's perky greeting was an octave too high. She was obviously trying to impress her new friends. "You remember Grace and Symone?"

Teegan stuck out her hand, but I had to force my smile. I grabbed a water bottle from my bag before I said something I'd later regret.

"So glad you're part of the guard, Mia." They waved in unison before taking off. "You fit right in with us."

I spurted out the water in my mouth.

Mia turned as bright red as her towel.

"What?" Teegan's brows furrowed. "When did you try out?"

"Uh, a few weeks ago." Mia bit her lip. "I was going to tell you."

Teegan crossed her arms. "Since when do we keep secrets?"

Hoot shifted her weight. She hated conflict as much as animal cruelty.

Mia's eyes flashed. "Since I knew you'd try to talk me out of try-outs." Her accent got strong when fueled by anger or nervous energy.

Confusion crossed Teegan's face. "Why would I do that?"

I winced. This conversation was headed for disaster. As soon as she mentioned the "b" word, Teegan would explode.

Mia straightened her shoulders. "Because I'm not going out for basketball in high school. Basketball is your dream. I'm ready for a change."

The words hit Teegan like a force field. She nearly toppled over from the impact. She could only blink in stunned silence.

"Now's probably not the best time to congratulate you, huh?" Bing tried to lighten the mood.

Teegan growled, and Mia muttered something in Spanish.

"Want to hit the lazy river?" Hoot—ever the peacemaker—pulled on Bing's elbow before the fireworks exploded. "You coming with us, Rooster?"

Exiting the scene was a no brainer. The last thing I wanted was to get in the middle of an argument on my birthday.

***

Avoiding Oliver became impossible. His youth group volunteered once a week at the shelter over the summer, and he never missed a session.

He wasn't the girls, but Bronwyn liked his company. She told herself not to get close. But it was hard to distance herself. He was the highlight of her week.

If Oliver didn't have a joke, he had a random fact to share from the science or history channels. His quirky personality wouldn't win him a popularity contest, but Oliver was comfortable in his own skin. And he never pressured Bronwyn to divulge her past.

"You intrigue me, mystery girl." He dunked his hands in soapy water to clean a pan from the lunch rush. "Are you an heiress with a hidden fortune or the daughter of some foreign dignitary seeking political asylum?"

133

She scraped another dirty pan and let his imagination run crazy. Once Oliver entertained her with the saga of her prowess as a superhero. Another time he spun a tale of Bronwyn's secret life wrangling wild mustangs from captivity. The stories Oliver wove were far more amusing than the ugly truth.

"I'm going to crack your silence someday," he promised. "Just you watch."

Bronwyn laughed. She needed to talk to the girls. They would help her figure out her growing feelings for Oliver—feelings she was trying desperately to avoid and failing miserably.

"So are you ever going to give me your number so we can text each other?"

The youth group leader called out to Oliver, saving Bronwyn. She didn't want to admit not having a phone.

"Next week." Oliver waved before he got in the van.

Bronwyn exhaled. How could she avoid his questions? Oliver had no idea she lived at the shelter for women and children. The thought of his pity was enough to keep her silent.

She longed to hang out at the lake with Oliver. What could one day hurt away from the monotony of her summer at the mission? Bronwyn could almost feel the sun kiss her flesh.

Her smile disappeared when reality hit. What was she thinking? Bronwyn didn't have a normal life. They were homeless.

What happened when her father found them, and they had to run again?

Oliver was better without her.

Chapter Eleven

I clutched the Maj's letter in one hand and shut the mailbox with my hip. Petey pulled on his leash as I prodded him toward the front door.

"Don't even start pouting." I opened the screen. "We just spent the last hour on a walk."

I tore into the envelope and yanked out the letter, catching the faintest hint of incense mixed with dirt. Petey sat on his haunches and barked, waiting for me to read out loud. I swear the dog loved mail call as much as me.

"Okay, okay." A giddy laugh escaped my lips. "I'll read it." Something about holding mail from the Maj made him feel closer. Even if a dozen people handled the envelope, the last person to touch the actual letter was my dad.

Hey Rooster,

Did I ever tell you that I can see ruins from an old outpost of Alexander the Great on the mountains surrounding my qalat? In quieter moments, I find myself wondering how different life was centuries ago.

I wish you could visit the marketplace with me or taste some of the traditional food here. Naan is this delicious flat bread that makes my mouth water just writing about it. One of the local Afghan translators brought me some creamed honey to spread over the Naan—yum!

Thank you for sending supplies to make s'mores. Wrapping the chocolate in bubble wrap was genius. The Hershey's bars arrived in perfect condition. And the same translator got a kick out of eating our gourmet camping dessert. He ate five!

Popcorn has been fun, too. I made some in the Whirley Pop popcorn popper you and Mom sent for Father's Day, and the local officials are hooked. When I leave, I'm going to leave the popper with the director of agriculture here as a gift. He and I have met many times in our mission to help develop a stronger agricultural economy.

Porter, the sergeant major, is practicing for his first marathon when he returns home, so a bunch of us have upped our workouts and started counting our miles. It's more for bragging rights, but motivation always helps. I almost broke my foot on the rocky terrain yesterday morning, but otherwise, your old man isn't doing too bad. I'm in third place right now.

We adopted a stray yellow lab the soldiers named Gunner. He's a scrappy thing with a stubby tail, but smart and loyal. The dog is good for us—a reminder of home.

I think of you, Colter, and Mom all the time.

Love, Dad

Petey cocked his head when I read the part about the stray yellow lab.

"Don't be jealous." I stroked his head, and he licked my face. "You're still Maj's favorite."

"Any good mail?" Mom asked as she grabbed her keys. "I'm going to a movie with Teegan's mom."

I handed her a second letter from the Maj, happy that she was doing something for herself and grateful for friends who got it. A lot of people made empty promises when the Maj left, but few acted.

My mom never asked for help even when desperation hit. When the Maj left for Iraq the first time, she tore her ACL at the gym and drove herself to the emergency room. If Teegan's mom hadn't organized help from the neighbors to bring over meals, shovel the snow, and take me to preschool, Mom would've ended up in a body cast from hobbling around, trying to do everything by herself. The same grit that made her a great soldier's wife made asking for help hard.

"Have fun." I chugged a bottle of water.

She hugged the Maj's letter and stuck it in her purse before heading out the door. I needed to pack. I was headed to my grandparents' house for a month, and then a week-long military kids' wilderness camp after that. I would get home the day before summer basketball camp started.

Petey trotted after me as I gathered an old rucksack I'd inherited from the Maj to use for the wilderness camp. Mom's suitcase would be perfect for the time with my grandparents.

"Don't look so sad." I grabbed a pile of clean clothes from the laundry room. "I'll miss you and the girls, too."

Petey plopped on my bed and rested his face in his paws.

137

"Don't give me those eyes." I stuck a pair of camouflage capris into the suitcase along with Riley. No way would I leave my beloved bear behind. "I didn't ask to leave. Mom wants to keep me busy over the summer so I don't have time to miss the Maj."

Petey covered his face with a paw.

"I wish you could go, too." I took his head in my hands. "Teegan promised to take you to the dog park while I'm gone."

My words didn't make a difference. Petey's blues were contagious.

"Scoot over." I nudged Petey's massive body to make room on the bed and stroked his head. "Why do adults always think we need to keep busy?"

Petey barked in agreement.

"I mean, what's wrong with binging on Netflix and hanging with the girls all summer?" We sat under my jungle netting until the doorbell ended my complaining session.

"Go away," I muttered, but the chime turned to a rain of pebbles against my window pane. I opened the latch and peered through the branches of the burr oak which stood between my house and Teegan's.

"You okay?" Hoot called up to me. "We got worried when you didn't answer."

I could've gone out the front door, but climbing into the tree was much more fun. The earthy smell of leaves and bark wrapped me in a dozen memories.

I paused at a familiar fork in the branches where Colter had shaved off the bark with his first pocket knife—a Christmas gift from the Maj—and engraved our initials. Time had darkened the letters, but not the moment etched in my mind. I could still see

Colter, legs straddling a large branch, as he dug the blade into the woody flesh.

My brother was fearless as he taught me to scale the branches and swing from a rope he'd rigged from an upper limb so we could become Tarzan and Jane. A broken arm had nearly ended our play, but the Maj convinced Mom that every kid needed a climbing tree.

I jumped off the last branch, and my dog tags clinked as I landed in the middle of the girls. The thought of not seeing them for five weeks nearly killed me. The summer would practically be over when I returned.

"Do you really have to go?" Mia frowned. She'd confided in me her fear that the tension between her and Teegan would accelerate without me to diffuse the situation. The only reason they didn't get into a huge fight at the water park was because they didn't want to ruin my birthday.

"You could hide out in my room," Bing interjected. "No one would find you in the mess."

I couldn't help but laugh.

"When does your flight leave?" Teegan adjusted her ball cap.

"Tonight."

"So we have time to collect on a rain check?"

"Rain check?" Hoot knit her eyebrows.

"On a tub of ice cream." Teegan's look dared me to tell more.

"Thanks, big mouth." I pushed her shoulder. It was impossible to hide anything from the girls.

"Spill it." Mia crossed her arms and clicked her manicured nails against her brown flesh. "You know the rules. No secrets."

"Fine." I rushed before Teegan could take a jab at Mia for keeping guard try-outs a secret. "The Maj left me clues for a yearlong treasure hunt. Big mouth saw me finding one of the caches."

"As in geocaches?" Light glinted off Hoot's braces. Neon pink and purple bands replaced the school colors.

I nodded. "Yeah. The Maj thought it would help pass the time."

"And you wanted to keep it to yourself?" Understanding pooled in Hoot's dark eyes. "Sorry we ruined it."

"You didn't." I grinned. It would be fun to have the girls help since I'd be gone so long. "Wanna find the next cache with me?"

"Do we still get ice cream?" Bing bounced in front of me. She never forgot the promise of sugar.

I grinned. "Definitely."

After retrieving money, the GPS, and the envelope, I read the sixth clue to the girls. "Books and schedules, games and memories. Four years passes too fast."

"High school?" Teegan ventured a guess.

"Likely." I turned on the GPS, and Mia took the envelope which read "procrastination."

"What does that mean?"

"The theme. Each cache has a challenge from the Maj."

We headed toward the high school, and I told them about the African proverb and the ice cream challenge.

Bing licked her lips. "I like this treasure hunt already."

"Don't forget," Teegan piped up. "We can't use bowls."

The streets in our neighborhood weren't busy, so we walked side by side, the sun casting our shadows in front of us. I took a mental picture of the silhouettes of my friends, wondering how much we'd change over high school.

The building was locked, so we slipped through a side door when a janitor did a trash run. The empty halls were too quiet, making me feel like I was trespassing.

"Why do I feel like we're breaking the rules?" Hoot whispered.

"Maybe because schools are just creepy in the summer." Bing trembled, and her curls shook.

Our flip flops clicked against the linoleum. No amount of camouflage—including the print on the tank top I wore with my shorts—would blend in with the stark walls of the school if a staff member found the five of us wandering the halls.

"I'm guessing the gym." Teegan didn't bother to lower her voice. She was the only one who felt comfortable. The high school was her home away from home with her dad as a coach and teacher. "I bet our dads teamed up on this clue together."

I glanced at the GPS screen and figured Teegan had to be right. We passed the locker rooms and stepped into the empty gym. Shadows would make our search challenging.

"Can we turn on the lights?" Mia asked.

I eyed the bleachers. Overhead lights wouldn't help if the geocache was underneath one of the seats. "Use the flashlight on your phone."

"There's a hound dog at the shelter who could pick up the scent in no time." Hoot put her hands on her hips. "What exactly are we looking for?"

141

"Anything. A cache can be as big as a plastic tub or as tiny as a screw head."

"Well that narrows it down." Mia snorted. "This could take forever."

"Especially if he hid it under one of the bleachers," Teegan voiced my thoughts.

Bing blinded me with the light on her phone.

"That way." I put my hands on her shoulders and pointed her body toward the bleachers. She clomped up the steps, the ring of metal bouncing off the walls.

"Quiet," Hoot hissed at Bing. "You're as loud as Jellybean when he's hungry. This is a covert operation."

Mia scanned the bleachers. "So did the Maj have a favorite section?"

"You're a genius." I snapped my fingers. "Center court. Tenth row. The number on my brother's jersey when he played in high school."

Leave it to Mia to solve the challenge. The girl was a brain even if she didn't like to admit it. We counted off the bleachers and spread across the center of the tenth row.

"Run your fingers underneath the seat," I explained. "We'll probably find something magnetic."

The air conditioning unit kicked on, humming in the background as we began our search. Anticipation made time slow until Bing burst out. "I found something."

"What are you girls doing?" a voice boomed at the same time, making me jump. I hurried toward Bing and plucked the small magnetic key box in my pocket. Something rattled inside.

"Hey, Mr. Harvey," Teegan greeted the custodian. "My dad thought he left a coaching manual in the stands. Did you see a blue binder?"

Mr. Harvey leaned on his dust mop. "Haven't seen anything, but I'll keep a look out."

"Thanks." She jumped off the last step. "You ready, girls?"

We filed past Mr. Harvey, giving short waves and quick goodbyes. We barely made it out of earshot when nervous laughter took over.

"Thanks for saving us, Teegan." I gave her a fist bump. "We don't want to start high school with detention."

"Tell me about it." She rolled her eyes. "It's gonna be hard enough having my dad as a teacher. I won't get away with anything."

"So what's in the box?" Bing couldn't hold her curiosity.

I took the box from my pocket and slid off the lid. Our five heads touched as we peered at a graduation tassel resting on top of a piece of folded paper.

"What's it say?" Hoot asked as I pulled it from the box.

"Four years of high school will be gone in a blink of an eye," I read. "Challenge #6: Try new things. Don't let procrastination steal the gift each day offers."

"Sounds like an invitation for ice cream to me," Bing batted her eyelids, reminding me of my earlier promise.

I grinned. "With chocolate and marshmallows."

She let out a whoop and did a cartwheel.

"What are you doing?" Teegan pulled Bing toward the door. "How am I going to explain your acrobatics to Mr. Harvey?"

A grin spread across my face as I hurried after the others toward the Kwik Shop. Geocaching was even more of an adventure with my crazy friends.

Twenty minutes later we sat on the merry-go-round at the park armed with five plastic spoons and a tub of Rocky Road ice cream between us.

"This whole thing sounds exactly like something Coach would do," Mia reflected.

"Whatever it is." Bing chewed on a marshmallow. "Your dad's pretty cool."

I smiled, letting my leg trail off the merry-go-round.

Mia put the lid on the ice cream and laid back against the metal. "Remember when we used to come here as kids?"

"We'd play for hours." Bing stretched out. "Look at the clouds. They look like cotton candy."

Hoot and Teegan leaned back, but I got hot with the sun beating down against the metal, so I stood and grasped the nearest bars. "Ready for a spin?"

Bing squealed in anticipation.

I ran until the momentum pushed me off. The girls blurred in front of me as laughter spun into the air. When the merry-go-round slowed, I hopped on and fell back against my friends. Our heads touched in the center, our hair spilling around us in different shades of color.

"Are we still spinning?" Hoot asked when we came to a complete stop. Sweat glistened on her dark skin.

I knew better than to sit up, but my phone chirped with a text message. I bolted up and regretted the movement immediately. Dizziness made the numbers swim in front of my eyes. I'd completely lost track of time. Mom was home from the movies and mad that I hadn't packed. "I gotta go." I hopped off the merry-go-round. "We're leaving for the airport in two hours."

The girls merged for a group hug before I sprinted home.

"We'll miss you," Teegan called out.

I couldn't look back. Otherwise, I'd never get on my plane.

***

"Higher!" Kenzie called out to Bronwyn as she leaned back on the swing and pumped her legs. The city park provided a welcome respite from the mission, especially with the hotter temperatures.

Mama sat on a nearby bench and read a mystery she'd borrowed from one of the teachers. She never had free weekends when she waitressed, so her relaxed expression was a nice change.

Bronwyn grabbed her sister's swing and ran underneath. She couldn't remember the last time she'd done an underdog.

Kenzie squealed in delight as the force pulled her higher. "Again!"

"One more time." The familiar thud of a basketball drew Bronwyn's attention to the court where a group of kids had gathered to play. Their faces blurred, and she saw Hoot wave her arms to block Teegan's jump shot. Rooster snagged the ball on the rebound and took off down the court with Bing and Mia on her tail.

"Are you going to play basketball?" Kenzie broke her thoughts.

Bronwyn shook her head, and the girls vanished from her mind.

"But you love basketball."

"Maybe next time."

Kenzie jumped off the swing and joined a group playing on the monkey bars. Why couldn't she be as fearless as her sister when it came to making friends?

Bronwyn wrapped her fingers around the cold metal chain and watched the game from her vantage point. Distance was safest at this point.

"You should join them." Mama looked up from her book and nodded toward the basketball court.

Bronwyn took a seat. "Not today."

Mama didn't argue. "Have you made any friends here yet?"

Bronwyn didn't mention Oliver. She'd avoided him for the past three weeks. Missing him was hard enough.

Mama closed her book and pulled Bronwyn close, filling her with the smell of freshly washed hair. The warmth of the embrace soothed the silence.

Bronwyn's stomach grumbled.

"Let's grab something from one of the food stands along the river," Mama suggested. "I still owe Kenzie an ice cream cone."

Bronwyn raised her eyebrows, but Mama brushed aside her concern. "We can splurge this once. I almost have the deposit saved for an apartment."

Kenzie trotted to the bench when Mama called her, and they meandered along the sidewalk that followed the river. A rowing club practiced on the water, their oars breaking the indigo surface in rhythmic precision. A family of ducks quacked along the bank.

Mama had enough for hot dogs and ice cream which made Kenzie squeal in delight. They tossed rocks into the river before twilight fell.

They climbed the stairs at the bridge, and the blare of car horns broke the peaceful spell. High rise buildings choked Bronwyn. The city made it easier to hide. But she missed small town life.

They passed walls painted in graffiti as they neared the mission. Bronwyn gasped at the familiar figure slumped against the wall. She hadn't seen Weather since the cold spell when they'd slept at the church.

"Oh my goodness." Mama rushed forward and knelt beside the girl. "Weather?"

Weather turned a bloody face to Mama, and Bronwyn felt her stomach lurch. An ugly black bruise ringed a swollen eye, and a gash ran the length of her forehead. Kenzie sobbed, so Bronwyn pulled her sister close. The little girl had never seen Mama's bruises. She was just a baby when they'd fled their father.

"Where does it hurt?" Mama tucked a stray lock behind Weather's ear. "Can you stand up?"

Weather winced. "Maybe, if you help me."

Mama wrapped Weather's arm around her shoulder and helped her to her feet. Her stomach bulged from under her shirt. "Easy. Don't overdo it."

Weather didn't groan despite the obvious pain. Bronwyn marveled at her strength.

"Do you think the baby's okay?" Weather stuttered. "He hit my stomach."

Mama gulped. "Who hit you?"

"My boyfriend."

Mama's lipped tightened. "Let's get you inside. Then we can call an ambulance."

147

Bronwyn held the door for Mama as she guided Weather inside the mission.

A few people looked at them, but said nothing.

"Go get one of the staff," Mama told Bronwyn as they stopped at a worn couch in the lobby. Volunteers didn't man the information desk after hours. "Kenzie, help me make Weather comfortable."

Bronwyn found Ms. Carmen outside the soup kitchen giving a tour to a small group of volunteers. Even though the crowd dwarfed her, the woman's non-stop activity made her larger than life.

"Excuse me." Bronwyn shifted her weight. Her face burned from interrupting the group, but she had to press past her discomfort. Weather needed her. "There's an emergency."

"Sorry to end the tour early," Ms. Carmen apologized to the group. "But this is exactly why we need your help. We depend on our volunteers."

Bronwyn filled Ms. Carmen in on the details as they hurried toward the lobby. Weather rested on the couch, her lips pressed to a water bottle Kenzie offered.

"The ambulance is on the way," Mama told Ms. Carmen. "Is there someone who can go with her?"

Ms. Carmen drummed her fingers together. "We're short-staffed as it is. I don't know if I can spare any of my help."

"Do you have any family?" Mama asked Weather.

When she shook her head, Kenzie clutched Bronwyn's hand tighter.

"What about a case worker?"

Weather tensed. "I'm not going into foster care."

Mama exchanged a look with Ms. Carmen who touched Weather's arm. "How old are you?"

148

"Old enough. My boyfriend and I are going to get married."

A siren screamed outside, ending all conversation and bringing a crowd of people from the shelter. Two medics rushed toward the couch, holding a stretcher.

Weather's eyes betrayed her fear as they lifted her from the couch.

"Go," Bronwyn told Mama. "Weather needs you. I'll keep an eye on Kenzie."

Mama frowned.

"We'll be fine." Bronwyn put on her brave face. She hated the thought of being without Mama, but she hated the thought of Weather being alone at the hospital more.

"Stay together." Mama gave Bronwyn and Kenzie quick hugs then boarded the ambulance behind Weather.

"She's pregnant." Mama didn't give the medic a chance to protest. "I'm the closest thing this girl has to family."

The medic didn't argue. He closed the door, and the ambulance howled toward the hospital.

Chapter Twelve

Somewhere over the Rockies, I was sandwiched between two snorers and bored with playing games on my iPod, so I flipped through the in-flight magazine. An advertisement for Jell-O made me think of Jada, and that's when the idea hit. What if Jada could go to the military kids' wilderness camp with me?

I'd call Mom as soon as I hit the ground. There were always last minute cancellations, and the donors who paid for military kids to attend camp wouldn't want any spots to go unfilled. I crossed my fingers. Jada didn't strike me as a wilderness adventure girl, but then again, I never pictured her training for a half marathon either, despite her runner's build. Camp might be just the thing to help Jada forget her pain—even if it was just for a week.

When I got off the airplane, my grandparents waited for me next to a life-sized cardboard cut-out of the Maj. His grin stretched from one corrugated ear to the other.

"Surprise." Poppy snapped a picture of my shocked reaction. "What do you think of your flat daddy? We ordered him online."

Staring into my dad's face was surreal. I didn't know if I should say something or salute. Some of our military friends had cut-outs of their soldiers, but I'd never been one to like attention. And standing next to a cardboard person made it hard to be inconspicuous.

"Welcome to Florida." My grandmother wrapped her arms around my waist. She gazed up at me with the same light blue eyes as my dad. "Either you're getting taller, or I'm shrinking."

I promised Mom I'd call as soon as I touched land, so I asked her about Jada when she got on the line. She couldn't talk much since she was at work, but she promised to check.

Lugging my flat daddy through the airport was awkward, and I got a lot of looks. But when people saw the camouflage hat and uniform, smiles lit up their faces. Pride radiated through me.

Maybe I'd bring my flat daddy to my basketball games if I made the high school team. I'd seen our military friends take selfies and other goofy pictures with their flat daddies at everything from birthday parties to ballet recitals—anything the soldier missed. Silly, but a fun way to show the soldier was present in spirit.

"Excuse me." Someone in the crowd stopped me and pointed to my flat daddy. "Is your father deployed with the military overseas?"

I hesitated, not sure how much I should reveal to the stranger.

The woman sensed my hesitation and pulled out her identification badge as a news reporter. She wanted to do a feature story for the local newspaper.

I didn't know what to say until my grandparents nodded their approval. Why not? The Maj would probably get a kick out of it. And Mom could add the article to her deployment scrapbook.

151

The reporter motioned toward a coffee shop, so we moved out of the flow of traffic. She asked me questions about the deployment and then ended by taking a picture of me with my flat daddy.

Two days later at the beach with my grandparents, a newspaper rack in a convenience store caught my attention. The Maj's cardboard clone and I made the front page of the living section. The woman at the counter recognized me from the picture when we bought several copies.

"Nice article." She didn't charge me for the candy bar. "That's on me. Thanks for your sacrifices."

I was used to people thanking the Maj, but couldn't remember anyone expressing their gratitude to me—a kid.

My grandfather put his arm around me when we walked out of the store, and his voice got husky. "She's right, you know. Military families are the real unsung heroes."

He didn't voice his fears, but I knew he and my grandmother worried about my dad. Fighting in Vietnam was a subject my grandfather rarely mentioned. The Maj told me antiwar protestors called Poppy a baby killer when he returned home and even spit in his face.

"I've never really thanked you for your service." I leaned into Poppy's embrace. "I'm sorry America didn't give you more respect when you came home from Vietnam."

A single tear slipped down his cheek. I'd never seen my grandfather cry.

***

I couldn't sleep later that night, so I slipped into the Maj's old room and flipped on the desk lamp. My grandparents converted it to an office, but remnants of my dad's childhood adorned the walls. An old baseball rested on a shelf while a shadow box framed a high school basketball jersey. If I inhaled deeply, I could almost smell sweat and victory.

I sat in the desk chair and tucked my legs under me. Old pictures lined the walls, bringing a familiar ache. The Maj holding a large catfish, his toothless grin stretching ear to ear. A candid family shot of the Maj and his siblings under the Christmas tree, all five dressed in matching footed pajamas. Poppy and the Maj in front of a tent on a camping trip in the mountains.

A lone picture on top of the worn desk caught my eye. Poppy stood next to the Maj while my mom stood on his opposite side. Each pinned a bronze oak leaf cluster on his shoulder for his promotion to major.

The sadness at the edge of my consciousness grew until it filled the room. The quiet magnified the Maj's absence. I longed to hear his deep voice and talk about nothing. And everything.

I tried to push aside thoughts of roadside bombs and terrorists, but I couldn't ignore the constant threat especially with the warm weather. Fighting escalated during the spring and summer. Was the Maj in the middle of a mission? Being "outside the wire" increased the danger.

My heart started to race, so I gulped in deep breaths. Panic attacks were the worst. Last time the Maj deployed I ended up in the emergency room because I couldn't stop shaking.

Peaceful thoughts. My eyes roved the office walls again, looking for another memory to anchor me. A faded picture showed the Maj dressed up as a heavy metal rocker for a costume party. He strummed a blow-up guitar, wearing earrings and a flowing black wig. Other than his muscles bulging from a sleeveless shirt, I wouldn't have recognized him. The long hair was so different than his normal buzz cut.

I laughed out loud, and my grandfather peeked his head into the room. Tousled white hair stuck up in multiple directions.

"Sorry." I touched my hand to my lips. "Did I wake you?"

"No. I saw the light." Poppy took a seat on the rocking chair in the corner. "I get up once or twice a night to move around. My body groans a lot more the older I get."

"What's your excuse?" His mustache wiggled when he grinned. "You're too young for your body to be complaining."

I swung my legs from under me. "I don't know. Couldn't sleep."

"Want some leftover pizza?" He winked. "Just don't tell Grandma. It's not good for my heartburn."

I poured myself a glass of water while Poppy took the pizza box from the refrigerator.

"Cold or warmed up?"

I took a piece of cold pepperoni pizza, and we took seats at the counter.

"What do you think your dad's doing right now?" Poppy grabbed a napkin.

"Maybe eating, too." I bit into my pizza. "Did he tell you about surf and turf nights?"

Poppy shook his head. "Beats the shelf-stable stuff I ate out in the jungle. I lost ten pounds overseas."

An hour disappeared as he told me stories I'd never heard from his days in Vietnam—his first ride on a helicopter, a friendly monkey who hung out in the trees above his hammock, and a friend who carved yo-yos out of wood and gave them to the local kids.

My eyes got heavy, but I wanted to hear more. When I stifled a yawn, Poppy finally called it a night.

"It's been a long time since I talked about those days." We walked down the hall. "Thanks for listening to your old Poppy."

As I crawled under my camouflage blanket, I couldn't help but wonder about the Maj. When he got home, what memories would keep him up at night? Would he be haunted by nightmares?

***

Two weeks later, pine straw crunched under my feet and sweetened the air as I followed Tressa, my camp counselor, and the other girls toward our cabin. Laughter rose from the cabin groups ahead of us while song birds darted between the canopy of branches.

I shifted the weight of my rucksack. The thing had to be at least ten pounds heavier thanks to the bucket load of junk food my grandparents sent with me. Good thing Jada was able to come. I needed someone to help me eat the entire stash. Even though Jada was petite, I hoped she had a big appetite, or at least, a sweet tooth.

She trekked through the trees next to me, her gaze taking in every detail—the undergrowth of ferns and wild flowers, the moss-covered bark, the cloudless sky overhead and the mountains which surrounded us.

"Have you ever been to summer camp?" I tried to make small talk. Jada had been quiet ever since she'd arrived an hour earlier.

She shook her head. "I've never been anywhere." Jada still seemed a bit shocked that a spot had opened for her after a last minute cancellation. The week promised tons of fun—zip lining, trail riding, a challenge course, fishing, swimming. I couldn't wait.

"You're going to have tons of fun." Tressa beamed, her brown eyes bright. Long braids peeked from beneath her yellow bandana. "Look. We're at the cabins."

The foot path ended at six log cabins which formed a semi-circle around a fire ring. Colored flags identified each group. Girls scattered around us as we followed Tressa up the steps to our cabin.

"Welcome to the yellow cabin." She fanned her hand toward a room filled with four metal bunkbeds. An open door in the corner led to a bathroom with two sinks and two shower stalls. "Claim your bunks. This is your home away from home for the next six nights."

"Dibs on the top bunk," two voices called out at the same time.

I turned to Jada. "Top or bottom?"

She claimed the bottom, so I tossed my rucksack on the top bunk. We only had a half hour before our first activity—rock climbing.

"No flip flops, girls." Tressa handed out bandanas to each of us. "You need closed toe shoes for the rocks."

I tightened my ponytail and tied my bandana around my head. Jada had trouble with hers, so I offered to help.

"Mia would be proud." I stood back and admired the French braid which fell to her shoulders. "You look cute."

Jada's eyebrows raised in disbelief under her glasses.

"Come see." I pulled her to the mirror and watched her surprise turn to a smile when she saw her reflection. The bandana framed the heart-shaped face normally hidden behind her shaggy locks.

"So you're really training for a half marathon?" I asked as we headed out the door after the others.

Jada's eyes got big. "Who told you that?"

I reddened, realizing my mistake. I either had to lie or admit hearing her mother speak about homelessness. I decided to tell the truth.

"I heard your mom speak."

Jada's face dropped. "Oh."

I wanted to kick myself. Jada had peeked out of her shell. The last thing I wanted was for her to disappear again. "I'm sorry. Your secret's safe with me."

"It's okay." She sighed. "I have to get comfortable with my story if my mom and I want to raise awareness about PTSD."

"That's really brave."

"Thanks." She wrinkled her nose. "I'm better at hiding."

Seventy-two hours later, Jada was a different person. She flew down the double zip line like a pro and grinned the entire trail ride on a mare named Clover. I found out she had a stamp collection and an obsession for strawberry Twizzlers. Jada loved to bake and wanted to be a chef someday. She didn't even complain when our cabin had KP duty. She practically sang when she mopped the kitchen floors. The girls wouldn't believe me if I told them about her transformation.

The only time she showed any fear was when we headed to the lake to canoe. The sun sparkled off the water, making me want to take a dip, but Jada frowned.

"What if we tip?" She stared at the lake. "That's a long swim back."

"This will keep you floating." I handed her a life jacket. "Plus, I've been canoeing since I was in kindergarten. My dad got me a kayak for my seventh birthday."

Jada was impressed, but it still took me almost ten minutes to coax her into the canoe. Tressa pushed us off shore.

The canoe wobbled, and the blood drained from Jada's face. "Uh, maybe we should turn back."

"It'll get better," I promised. "Trust me."

Jada gripped the sides.

I dipped the oar into the water, and the canoe sliced through the lake with my rhythm.

Eventually Jada let go of her death grip on the sides and relaxed. A hawk circled overhead, and a fish splashed to our side.

"Look." I pointed to a turtle swimming alongside us. His head skimmed the water.

"He reminds me of Wellington." Jada smiled.

"Who's Wellington?"

"My brother's turtle." As soon as the words left her lips, I could see the regret. Jada hadn't talked about Jason once during camp.

"I'm sorry about your brother." I stopped paddling and let the canoe drift. "I heard he was a good soldier."

Realization hit Jada. "Your dad was the one who helped my parents, wasn't he?"

I nodded. "I connected the pieces together that day you showed me Jason's picture."

"Battle changed my brother."

I gulped, thinking of the Maj.

"When Jason came home for two weeks, he was distant and angry." Jada got a far-off look. "Nightmares haunted him day and night. My mom tried to convince him to get help, but he brushed it off."

I traced the wood grain in the oar with my finger, not sure what to say.

"I miss him so much." Tears filled her eyes. "He was annoying like older brothers are, but I'd give anything to see him again."

159

The water lapped against the sides of the canoe gently rocking us, but Jada's earlier fear was gone.

"It's the little things I miss the most. Making goofy faces at each other, fighting over who got shotgun, and the water wars that erupted whenever we washed the dog."

I felt the same way about the Maj. Some days I went crazy wondering if I'd ever see him again.

"Remembering hurts." A sad smile crossed Jada's face. "But it feels good, too."

A whistle pierced the air. Tressa waved her hands from the dock, signaling us to head back to shore.

"Supper time."

Jada grabbed an oar. "So how do you work this thing?"

"Really?" I raised my eyebrows.

"Really." She dipped the oar into the water, and I showed her how to paddle. We circled toward the left before we got straightened out and paddled in sync. Jada gave a shout of victory.

"You catch on fast."

She grinned. "I almost didn't come to camp," Jada admitted as we pulled up next to the pier. "But I'm glad I did."

"Me, too." I hopped out of the canoe and reached to help her.

Jada grasped my arm and gratitude filled her eyes. "Thanks for inviting me."

***

Kenzie's deep breathing helped calm Bronwyn. She pictured Weather at Kenzie's age—a girl who jumped rope and climbed trees and dreamed of a bright future, not life on the streets.

How could Weather care for a child? She couldn't even care for herself.

A noise made Bronwyn strain her eyes. A penlight cast a beam of light in the darkness, blinding her to the body shuffling toward them. She clutched her sister.

"Bronwyn?" Mama whispered. "Are you awake? I'm back from the hospital."

Bronwyn sat up, relief flooding her. Mama sat on the edge of the bed and kissed Kenzie's cheek before squeezing Bronwyn's hand.

"How's Weather?" She kept her voice low.

"She broke a couple ribs, and the doctor stitched the gash on her forehead." Mama loosened a shoelace and rubbed the top of her foot.

"Is Weather still at the hospital?"

Mama shook her head. "The hospital released her to a case worker from social services."

"But she doesn't want to be in foster care."

Mama's lips tightened. "It's safer than the alternative."

Bronwyn narrowed her eyes. "What about the baby?"

"She lost the little guy." Mama's expression was grim. "The state will file charges. Her boyfriend is headed to jail. He's bad news. Really bad news."

Bronwyn forced down the bile that rose to her throat. Revulsion mixed with her anger. She wanted to cover her ears, push out the things she didn't want to hear. The ugly reality for girls like Weather.

"Will we see her again?"

Mama exhaled. "I hope not, for Weather's sake. The streets are no place for young girls."

Bronwyn couldn't help but shudder as she stared at her sister. Kenzie slept soundly, completely oblivious to the fears that crept into her nightmares.

Her father was no different than Weather's boyfriend. How long till he found them in the city? Would they ever be safe?

Chapter Thirteen
August 2012

The squeal fest lasted almost five minutes the second my mom pulled into our driveway which is funny considering Mia's the only real girly girl in our group. We couldn't help the excitement that bubbled over. Five weeks apart was a record for us.

"How was camp? Did you meet any cute guys? What'd you bring us?" Questions peppered the air as we exchanged hugs and news. Hoot and Collin had broken up, but decided to remain friends. Mia's large extended family grew by three new baby cousins. Bing's mom got remarried. And Teegan was brown from spending the afternoons at the pool with Savanah. No one believed me when I showed them pictures of Jada.

"That's Jada?" Mia grabbed my phone and stared at a picture of the two of us on the swinging rope bridge at camp. "Her braids look adorable."

"I've never seen her smile." Hoot grinned. "She looks so happy."

Mom opened the front door, and Petey bounded outside and into my arms. He licked my face until I was drenched with slobber.

"Good to see you, too." I hugged his neck.

Mom grabbed my bag from the trunk. "I'm going to start some laundry so you have clean clothes for basketball camp tomorrow."

I swallowed a groan. I needed a week of sleep. How was I going to survive five days of drills and conditioning?

"Can you believe it's finally here?" Teegan lit up. "One of our coaches used to play with the Harlem Globetrotters."

"No way." Bing jumped up like she was going for a pretend shot and toppled into Hoot. They landed in a pile on the grass.

"Save that move for tomorrow." Teegan reached out her hand. "We're going to breathe basketball 24-7."

I managed a weak smile. I just wanted sleep.

***

I growled at my alarm the next morning. We didn't even wake up this early at camp.

When the doorbell blared, I stumbled toward the front door. Teegan looked like a kid at Christmas.

"Wake up, Sleeping Beauty." She barged into the house. "What do you want for breakfast? We're leaving in ten."

"I'm not hungry."

"You need fuel." She sounded like Coach. "Breakfast bar? Toast? What sounds good?"

"Sleep." I fell on the couch. Mom had already left for the hospital.

Teegan grabbed a protein bar and pulled a pair of basketball shorts from the drier. "Get dressed unless you're going in your pajamas."

I eyed my camo flannels. "Works for me."

"Very funny."

I wasn't joking, but Teegan was determined to get me out of the door. The girl should join the Army. She was a regular drill sergeant.

Fifteen minutes later, we walked onto the college campus and found the gym. Girls who sported shirts from the Remington Rams and the Paulser Panthers, our school rivals, dribbled balls on the basketball court. If it weren't for the three friendly faces of Bing, Hoot, and Teegan, I might've bolted.

"Great," Teegan muttered when her eyes locked with a girl whose arms and legs appeared elastic. Everything about her was long, including her painted fingernails. "If it isn't Stretch."

The girl snarled at Teegan. "Nice to see you, too."

"Welcome to basketball camp, ladies." A man with an afro walked onto court and silenced any further confrontation. "I'm Coach Hassler, and this is my assistant, Coach Sandoz." A young guy with spiked hair waved. If Mia were at camp, she would've gone crazy over his bulging muscles.

"I hope you came prepared to sweat." Coach Hassler crossed his arms. "This week isn't for the faint of heart. Suicide drills are my favorite. Camp will be intense. Anyone who wants to back out, now's your chance."

The idea of profuse perspiration didn't appeal to me, but I didn't have the guts to do anything. Apparently neither did anyone else. No one moved the slightest muscle. This week would leave me begging for school to start.

165

Stretch and I got partnered together for two-man shooting drills. We took turns rebounding and shooting as we worked on everything from shot fakes and elbow shooting to crossovers.

When Coach Hassler blew his whistle, we had five minutes for a water break before he started the clock for the bird shooting drill—one of my favorites. Each shooter had two minutes to make two baskets in a row at each of nine positions—right corner, right wing, top, left wing, left corner, left wing, top, right wing, right corner.

"Nice." Stretch slapped my back when I finished the drill with 15 seconds to spare.

I could only nod between ragged breaths as we switched positions. Good thing I had on a tank top. I'd be pitted out in a t-shirt.

Stretch was a natural. The girl made the game look like a dance. I couldn't help but be impressed. Too bad she didn't play for Crawford. Stretch could bag us the state trophy.

"Good practice." Coach Hassler blew his whistle and corralled us for lunch. "Freshen up then head to the cafeteria."

My protein bar had long disappeared. The rumble in my stomach grew louder as we trudged from the gym to the cafeteria.

"Think we'll see Nick or Annie?" Teegan asked as we entered the building where we'd volunteered for Campus Kitchen.

"It's August." I took a tray. "Remember Annie said Campus Kitchen cuts back over the summer?"

Teegan's face fell, and I could read her thoughts. Hunger didn't know seasons. Empty stomachs growled day and night, spring and summer, fall and winter.

Bing cut in front of me, but a familiar voice stopped me before I could protest.

"Hey girls. What're you doing on campus?" Annie gave me a hug. She'd cut her hair in a cute bob.

"Basketball camp." Teegan beamed. "How are the wedding plans?"

"Giving the caterer our final numbers today." The notebook in her hand looked as detailed as her clipboard for Campus Kitchen. "The wedding is this weekend."

We wished her luck and told her about Coach's Cardboard City project.

"Good for you." Annie grinned. "Unless we get close to problems like hunger and homelessness, it's easy to forget about people hurting around us."

Coach Hassler and Coach Sandoz walked by with their trays, so we promised to keep in touch. We had to eat fast. The afternoon schedule sounded brutal.

"Remind me why we like basketball camp again?" I asked Teegan between bites of my hamburger.

"Because we want to be the best."

I groaned. "And why is that?"

"Because . . ." Teegan grinned. "Competitive is your middle name."

I couldn't argue. I could thank the Maj for that.

***

I made it as far as my couch where I crashed for three hours after practice. Petey sat on his haunches staring at me when I finally opened my eyes.

"What?" I laughed at him. "You miss me that much?"

Petey licked my face.

"Want to find the next geocache?" I dried my face on my shirt. "September is only a few days away."

My faithful pooch answered by bringing me his leash.

The seventh cache marked "catalyst" was at the park in the water fountain. I had to make sure no one was watching when I plucked a small waterproof container out of the fountain. Clear plastic made the box nearly invisible under water unless you were looking for something out of place.

"Clever, Maj," I mumbled when I opened the lid and found several pennies glued to the bottom. He'd rigged it so the coins looked like they were resting on the bottom of the fountain.

"Teegan would call this proof," I told Petey. She teased the Maj about being an undercover spy, especially when he couldn't reveal details about his travel. The pennies disguised the challenge which was written in permanent marker on the bottom of the container—an ingenious gadget obviously conceived by the mind of a secret agent.

"Someone once said, 'Be the change you wish to see in the world.' When you make a wish, wish to make a difference." Of course a penny rested inside the container.

Bubbles rose to the surface when I tossed the coin into the water and wished the summer didn't have to end. My first day of high school was a few days away, and I was a bundle of nerves.

Back at home, Mom pressed her fingertips to her temples and massaged her head.

"Bad day?" I grabbed a frozen pizza from the freezer.

"Multiple car pile-up." She rested her head in her hands. "I'm too tired to even eat."

"Take a long bath." I looked at the pile of dishes in the sink. "I'll clean up."

Mom exhaled. "You sure?"

I didn't tell her I was hoping we could talk. A lot had happened over the summer since I left for my grandparents. Even watching a movie together would be nice before school started, and life got busy with homework and classes.

"Thank you." She kissed the top of my head and disappeared to her room. "I really want to hear more about camp and basketball. Let's do supper out this weekend."

I hid my disappointment with a weak smile. I wanted to connect more with my mom, but our worlds spun in different orbits.

I finished the rest of my supper binging on Netflix when my phone buzzed. I smiled at the text from my brother. The Maj wasn't the only one I missed. I hadn't heard from Colter since he'd graduated from Airborne School.

"Hey, Freshie. Ready for high school?"

"Hey, Captain America."

A cartoon picture of an Army sergeant with an enlarged head and finger pointing at me flashed on my screen. "Are you being nice to Mom?"

"Trying. You staying out of trouble?"

"Trying," Colt mimicked me.

We went back and forth giving each other a hard time like old times until he had to go.

"Good luck on your first day. You'll do great."

I had my doubts, but I appreciated his vote of confidence. The Maj would say the same thing. "Thanks, bro."

"Later, Rooster. Lights out here."

"Miss you and your nasty toe jam smell," I signed off.

"Back at you, Fungus Breath."

"Butthead."

"Snot face."

"Zit pus."

"'Night, sis. Love you."

I sent an emoji hug. "Love you, too."

***

"Wait up," Oliver's voice reached Bronwyn's ears as she headed across the courtyard after school. She'd been dreading this conversation since she last saw Oliver at the mission. Bronwyn couldn't avoid him any longer now that school had started.

He jogged to her side and flashed a grin. "Hey. Did I do something wrong?"

She tried to ignore the sudden fluttering inside her. Oliver had shot up over the last month, gaining several inches over

170

her. His hair was shorter on the sides while gel managed the tousled curls on top. Contacts replaced his glasses, highlighting his blue-grey eyes.

"I never got your number. Then you stopped volunteering." He ran a nervous hand through his hair, springing a loose curl. "I missed you."

Bronwyn's mouth went dry. His confession shifted something inside. The same longing she'd felt with the girls hit her. Bronwyn wanted friendship. She was tired of being lonely. Tired of keeping up her guard. But what could she tell Oliver?

When Bronwyn didn't speak, Oliver changed the subject. "High school's a different beast, huh?" Spearmint gum mixed with his cologne. He'd never worn the stuff at the mission. "Are you taking any advanced classes?"

Bronwyn forced herself to recall her schedule. Could Oliver see the effect he was having on her? She needed some serious advice from Mia before she did something stupid. "Uh, biology and English."

"I looked for you at lunch." Oliver stuck his hands in the pockets of his jeans. "I have second. You?"

"First lunch."

Oliver didn't hide his disappointment. "Maybe we can study together sometime or hang out."

"I'd like that." Bronwyn smiled. She could imagine the girls cheering her on from the sidelines.

"Me, too." Oliver shuffled his feet in the awkward silence that followed.

Bronwyn didn't want to leave, but she needed to catch the city bus. "I gotta go."

"Do you want to go to Homecoming with me?" Oliver blurted out, and his face turned bright red.

The question stopped Bronwyn. The girls would be doing somersaults. She'd seen the fliers around school, but she'd never considered going herself.

Oliver leaned forward, waiting for her answer.

For just a second, Bronwyn felt like a character out of one of her sister's princess stories. But she didn't have a fairy godmother, and her friends weren't here to help. A dress was out of the question. Bronwyn couldn't pressure Mama—even if she'd gotten a long-term subbing job for a teacher on maternity leave this fall. Getting an apartment was their top priority.

"I can't," she rushed.

Oliver's face fell.

Bronwyn wanted to explain, but her own heart was breaking. She ran for the bus without looking back.

Fairy tales didn't come true for girls like her.

Chapter Fourteen
October 2012

I grabbed the eighth envelope and headed outside with Petey. Four weeks had already passed since I survived my first day of high school. Busy days left me little free time and itching to find the next geocache.

The GPS led downtown, pointing to the clock tower in the center of the square. I passed the bakery on the corner, and a dozen Saturday mornings with the Maj flooded my mind. I saw the stool where I sipped my first coffee, which the Maj laced with sugar and milk. I spied the display case full of donuts and almost ordered our favorite—bear claws. A little girl with frosting on her face laughed as her father threatened to lick her cheeks. I bit my lip and hurried past. I would not cry.

Cars passed the intersection while I stared at the clock tower and formed my strategy. I didn't want any muggles watching. Should I pretend to be a tourist and take a picture, or should I return later under the cover of darkness?

My eyes roamed the area, trying to guess possible hiding spots. The hands of the clock would be an amazing spot, but highly unlikely. Getting inside the base of the tower would require a key for the door. The bricks could also be a possibility. Had the Maj found a notch to wedge in a small cache?

"Look natural," I muttered to Petey who responded by barking at another dog.

"Good boy." I patted his head. "That's the right idea. We want to blend in with the crowd."

He trotted beside me with confidence, bolstered by my praise. Halfway around the perimeter of the tower, a crack in the bricks caught my eye. I reached out my hand when a voice called out my name. My blood gelled.

I turned to see Mia wave from across the street. Symone and Grace flanked her either side. Both held shopping bags.

Getting discovered was bad enough. Sharing something so private with Mia's two new best friends made my anger flare. I had to think of an excuse fast.

"Hi, Mia." I jogged toward her. "What're you guys doing?"

"Shopping." Her accent betrayed her nerves. "Are you geocaching?"

As soon as the words slipped from her mouth, Mia knew she'd made a mistake. Red flooded her cheeks.

I jammed my hands in my pockets to avoid strangling her. How dare Mia share my secret?

Symone flipped her hair, completely unaware of our exchange. "What's geocaching?"

"Nothing," Mia twisted the bracelets on her arm, trying to backpedal.

"It's this stupid GPS hunt." Grace rolled her eyes. "My geek of a brother loves it."

My fingers curled in my pockets. Now I wanted to strangle Grace. The Maj and I were not geeks. Even Petey growled.

"Sounds lame." Symone turned to leave and stopped at the sight of her reflection in the glass of the shoe store they'd exited. Her satisfied smile only irritated me more. "My mom's waiting in the Lexus. Ready to head to the mall?"

Mia mouthed an apology, but the betrayal stung, making me frown. Symone and Grace had only entered the scene a few months earlier. How could Mia so easily dismiss our history?

I circled the block, trying to clear my head. Mia had missed Friday night's sleepover and sat with her new friends at the football game. Her excuse: the color guard's half-time performance. I had to agree with Teegan. The excuses would get old real fast. This latest slight definitely didn't help Mia's case.

I hurried to the clock tower, heading straight for the crack I'd noticed earlier. I thrust my hand forward and touched paper.

"I got something," my voice rose, exciting Petey. I pulled out a folded piece of paper.

We walked two blocks before I stopped at a bench in front of the public library. Petey sat on his haunches while I read the message.

"Being busy isn't always best. Too many people get distracted and lose sight of their dreams. Challenge #8: Spend a day doing nothing except dreaming. Dream big, and dream often."

I traced my finger along the word on the envelope. Distractions.

Like Mia and her new besties. Just the thought of them made my head throb.

Or the pile of homework I had to finish before Monday. Geometry was going to kill me.

Doing nothing sounded good to me.

"Challenge accepted." I smiled at Petey. A day without homework and chores was just the thing to get my mind off Mia and her betrayal.

***

The Maj's letter looked like it had been dragged through the mud. Water stains splotched the surface, making the address hard to read. It was amazing the letter even arrived. Mom always numbered her correspondence in case one got lost in the mail, but the Maj and I took our chances. When you really stopped to think about it, getting mail in and out of a war zone was pretty much a miracle.

Rooster,

Did your school have an assembly for 9/11? The soldiers here held a special flag folding ceremony to remember the day. I choked up seeing all those flags hoisted onto the pole and flying in the wind before being lowered and folded. Many of the guys joined the military because of what happened that day, so there weren't many dry eyes. I have a special flag for you and your brother when I get home. I'll send pictures as well.

Diablo's as ornery as ever. The stupid goat head-butted me in the stomach last week when I was helping the vet. I wanted to strangle the beast.

I worry about the local kids as the weather gets colder. Many of them run around without shoes. We have so much in America.

Thanks for your letters and care packages. Harrison's friend was touched that you sent him a package, too, since his grandmother lives in a nursing home, and he doesn't have any other family. Thoughts of home make the days easier.

Give Petey a hug and say "hi" to the girls.

Love, Dad

***

The room was typical Army boring. Linoleum flooring, white walls, plasterboard ceiling panels, and a recruiting poster framed by cheap plastic. Mom didn't miss a single family support session while I had made excuses for every meeting. Talking to a roomful of strangers was completely out of my comfort zone.

We sat on hard folding chairs in a circle united by one thing—deployment. I shifted my weight, already regretting the fact that I'd come. I should've never caved when Mom tossed in the guilt card.

She knew everyone. I only recognized Katrina. I kicked myself for not disappearing with the babysitters when I had the chance. They were in another room with the kids, playing games and doing crafts.

The MFLC quieted the room and welcomed everyone. The woman was basically a counselor with a fancy military acronym—Military Family Life Counselor. The chaplain sat to her right and gave a quick greeting.

I avoided eye contact. One of the spouses complained about a flooded basement. Another woman broke her arm. Mom looked more relaxed than I'd seen her for months. Knowing she wasn't alone meant everything.

"I'm tired of being tired," a petite woman with two toddlers confessed.

The MFLC gave her information about babysitters. "Call them," she urged. "You need downtime so Mama doesn't have a break down."

"Shopping trip," someone piped up, and the group laughed.

A dad shared his fears. A young wife talked about her loneliness. A girl my age wished her dad had been home to take homecoming pictures. Everyone had a chance to speak.

All eyes turned toward me.

"Uh, pass," I muttered and slumped in my chair. I didn't want to talk about my feelings or anything else.

Thankfully no one pushed me, or I would've bolted. Listening to the others was one thing. Sharing my heart wasn't gonna happen.

Someone yawned, which started a chain reaction.

The MFLC looked at the clock. It's late. "Thanks for sharing everyone. As always, you have my number if you need it."

Mom lingered to chat with Katrina. Large bags circled her eyes.

"Don't drive home," Mom insisted. "Stay at our house. You can make the two-hour trip home tomorrow."

Katrina hesitated only for a second. "Are you sure? I don't want Charlie to keep everyone up."

Mom brushed aside her concern. "I can sleep through anything. Besides, I need my baby fix."

Katrina eyed her son. "I'm so tired. He likes to play at night and sleep during the day."

I couldn't help but laugh at the big grin on Charlie's face. His cheeks had filled out since his days in the NICU. He was Gerber baby cute.

Back at our house, Mom lifted Charlie out of his car seat, and he kicked his legs at his freedom. He wore a camouflage sleeper that matched my long-sleeve t-shirt.

"Look at you." Mom erupted in a string of baby talk that would've been embarrassing in public. Charlie just grinned.

"He rolled over in his crib last night." Katrina beamed. "I tried to capture it on camera for Adam, but Charlie didn't do it again."

"You'll get another chance for a photo op." Mom tweaked Charlie's cheek. "This little man will be running in no time. You're going to be even busier than you are now."

Katrina exhaled. "I'll never make it."

"One milestone at a time." Mom shooed her toward the bedroom. "Take a long hot shower, then get some sleep. Josie and I will take care of Charlie."

Katrina couldn't hide her joy. "Really?"

"Go." Mom took the diaper bag. "Bottles in here?"

179

Charlie giggled when Petey bounded into the room and nuzzled his wet nose against him. Katrina made her getaway while he was distracted.

Mom grabbed us each a soda, and we headed for the living room to play with Charlie.

An hour and a diaper change later, he was still going strong, but Mom's eyes looked heavy.

"Go to sleep," I told her. "I can entertain Charlie."

"You sure?" Mom stumbled toward her room. "I'm more tired than I thought."

"I guess it's just you and me, kid." I bumped my fist against his, and he farted.

I laughed when Petey sniffed the air and moved away from the gaseous cloud. If the girls were here, we'd be rolling on the floor, dying of laughter. "I just changed your diaper."

"Smile, Charlie." I snapped a picture and sent it to Teegan. She and Savanah appeared at the door in minutes.

Savanah let out a muffled screech at the sight of Charlie and dropped to her knees beside him. He reached out for her, and she wrinkled her nose at the stench.

"Want to change his diaper?" I handed her the wipes.

"No way," she signed.

"No?" I mocked. "Don't you have to change the diapers on your dolls?"

She gave a vigorous shake of her head. I unsnapped Charlie's sleeper and tried not to inhale. I needed some rubber gloves. Charlie just cooed.

"Good thing you're so cute." I poked his belly, and he kicked his bare legs.

"I bet somebody's ticklish." Teegan brushed her fingers against Charlie's toes, and a giggle escaped his lips.

He looked so happy, I couldn't help but feel sorry for all the things his dad was missing. It was hard enough knowing everything the Maj missed in my life. But all the firsts happened in a baby's first year—crawling, teething, walking, first words.

Teegan must've been thinking the same thing. "It would kill me to be away from you." She lifted Charlie and propped him to a sitting position using the couch pillows. "How does your dad do it?"

Savanah laid on her stomach beside Charlie, and he giggled again. She made a face, and his giggle turned into a belly laugh. It was amazing how they connected even though Charlie couldn't talk and Savanah couldn't hear.

"He likes you." Teegan signed to her sister.

Savanah made another face, and Charlie almost tipped over from the force of his laughter.

I had to record this. I could just imagine Harrison watching this moment half a world away.

Savanah got sillier, and Charlie got louder. No wonder his mom never got any sleep. The kid was a night owl and a wannabe actor.

When I showed the video to Katrina and Mom the next morning, they replayed the footage three times.

"I've seen kids bond with each other." Mom stirred her coffee. "But Savanah has a gift."

I couldn't help but think of Savanah and Bronwyn's sister, Kenzie. The girls had become instant friends even with Savanah's hearing loss.

"Adam is going to love getting this video." Katrina hugged me. "It'll be a great surprise for his birthday. Thank you for everything."

I yawned. Charlie had finally fallen asleep three hours after midnight, long after Teegan and Savanah had gone home. And now he was conked out on a blanket on the floor beside an equally tired Petey. "Good night." I nodded to Mom and Katrina. "Wake me up for supper."

Laughter trailed behind me. I could barely lift my legs up the stairs. The Maj always said the battle was equally hard back home. I had to agree. Babies were exhausting.

***

Bronwyn hunched over the computer at the school library. It was easier to stay after school and work in the study lab than attempt homework at Hope's House. The computers were always in high demand.

"Five-minute warning," the librarian announced. "Time to shut down."

Several students headed for the door. Oliver packed up his books across the room, refusing to look Bronwyn's way. The sting hurt more than she wanted to admit. She resisted the urge to run after him. If only she could convince her heart it was better this way.

Bronwyn eyed the screen, wanting to beg for an extension. She still had another page to finish on her English essay which was due the following day.

Her fingers flew over the keyboard, but she could only get in one more paragraph. A late paper came with a penalty, and she worked hard to stay on the honor roll. Good grades were her chance for scholarships. She and Mama dreamed about her future—something far better than their current circumstances.

Bronwyn powered down the computer and stopped by the librarian's desk. A Garfield bobble head cat wobbled from the middle of a stack of books.

"Excuse me." Bronwyn cleared her throat. "What time do you open in the mornings?"

The librarian didn't make eye contact. "A half hour before the bell."

Bronwyn calculated the bus schedule in her head. She might have to leave before the shelter served breakfast, but she could make it work.

"Except tomorrow." The librarian clucked her tongue and looked at Bronwyn. "I almost forgot. The teachers have a staff meeting."

Bronwyn's face fell. She needed more than a half hour anyway.

"Sorry, kid." The librarian grabbed her keys and headed for the door. "I wish I didn't have to go to another meeting either."

Bronwyn managed a weak smile at the librarian's humor. She headed toward the bus stop, weighing her options. She only had enough bus fare for one trip. Which would it be—the public library or the shelter?

Her classmates complained about homework, but they had no clue what she endured just to turn in a simple assignment. Few who turned in late work even had a valid excuse.

So why did she care? Wouldn't it just be easier to take the zero and give up?

Bronwyn pushed out thoughts of quitting and boarded the bus for the public library. She hoped the rain would let up by the time she had to make the trek back to Hope's House.

A bearded man with black-rimmed glasses at the front desk asked how he could help.

"Do you have a phone I can use?" She would leave a message for Mama.

"Our office phones aren't for public use." He pursed thin lips. "You're welcome to use the pay phone at the front door. It's a relic. One of the few you'll see anymore."

"Thanks," Bronwyn muttered, not wanting to admit she didn't have change. "Do you have computers? I have an English essay to finish."

He pointed toward the elevators. "Third floor. West wing. You'll need a library card for access."

When Bronwyn hesitated, he handed her a form. "Fill this out to get a card."

Her heart sank at the standard questions. Bronwyn couldn't get a library card without an address.

"Never mind." She pushed back the paper. He'd probably recognize the address at the mission. And lying would eventually catch up with her. Mama would be worried anyway.

A gust of wind yanked the door out of her hands, biting Bronwyn's skin through her thin jacket. She hurried down the steps, avoiding the puddles in her path. At least the rain had stopped.

Bronwyn wanted to run, but the dinner hour crowded the sidewalks. Men and women in suits headed to parking garages and eating establishments. She turned south at the intersection and opted for the river trail. Except for a few runners and a fisherman, the trail proved empty.

Bronwyn jogged toward the mission, hoping it wasn't too late for dinner. Mama would be a mess of nerves.

When she neared the stairs at the bridge, the pungent smell of marijuana pricked her nostrils. A threesome shared a joint between them in the fading light. The two guys could've been linebackers. They dwarfed a third person who hunkered in the shadows.

Bronwyn slowed her pace, weighing her options. Avoiding the bridge was impossible without retracing her steps. Darkness loomed, pressing Bronwyn to get back to Hope's House. If Mama hadn't already called the cops, she would send out the National Guard.

The linebacker with the bad bleach job narrowed his eyes when he spied her.

She inhaled sharply and braced herself for the confrontation. He stepped in front of her to block her path. Bronwyn hugged her torso as his gaze roamed her body.

"Where are you going, sweet thang?"

She forced down the vomit that almost spewed and tried to sidestep his bulk.

"What?" His lip curled into a snarl. "You don't talk? Didn't your mama teach you better manners?"

"Please let me pass." Bronwyn shivered, trying to mask the tremble in her vocal chords. "I need to get home." She hesitated on the last word. The mission was far from home.

The second guy lumbered onto the path reeking of body odor and weed. Metal pierced his nose and tongue. "Don't you want to join our little party?"

Panic tightened Bronwyn's throat. His meaty hands could fit around her neck. Unless she could outrun the linebacker twins, Bronwyn could count the remaining seconds on her life. What was she thinking? If only she hadn't stopped at the library.

"Leave her alone." The faceless individual stuttered as she emerged from the shadows.

Shock rendered Bronwyn speechless at the sight of Weather.

"What are you doing out here alone?" A fresh gash on Weather's cheek mirrored the scar on her forehead. Dandruff flaked unkempt hair.

Bronwyn's heart sank. She could ask Weather the same thing. Had she run from her foster family only to escape one bad boyfriend for another?

"I, uh, had to go to the library for school," Bronwyn stammered.

"You making fun of my girl?" The guy with the piercings got in her face. "Weather can't help that she don't talk right."

"She's scared, Markus." Weather ran a hand along his arm until he relaxed. "Let me talk to her."

His cohort handed him another joint, and the two ambled back into the shadows.

Weather frowned. "The streets are dangerous. We'll walk you back to the mission."

Bronwyn didn't want anything to do with Markus or his friend, but she knew better than to argue. When they reached street level, Markus and his friend each took a side, sandwiching Bronwyn between them. She appreciated their protection when they passed a run-down house pulsing with music. Bodies spilled out of the front door and onto the street. A block later, they witnessed a drug deal between two thugs in an abandoned lot.

Something about Markus scared Bronwyn, but Ryne, the kid with the bad bleach job, was new to the streets. He stayed with friends and relatives after his dad went to prison then hit rock bottom when his mom overdosed. He was Bronwyn's age.

The sign above the mission illuminated the darkness. Bronwyn had never been so grateful to see the shelter.

"See you around." Weather waved without another word.

"Thanks." Bronwyn tried to say more, but Weather and her friends had already disappeared into the shadows.

She hurried into the mission where Mama paced the floor like a caged animal.

"Bronwyn?" Mama shrieked.

Kenzie jumped up from where she sat next to Ms. Carmen at the front desk.

"Where have you been? We've been worried sick." Mama crushed Bronwyn in her embrace. Kenzie joined the circle. "You're cold."

"I'm sorry." Bronwyn brushed away a tear that leaked from her eye. Seeing Mama and her sister made her realize how scared she'd been. "I had a paper to finish for English, so I went to the public library. I didn't have money for the pay phone."

Ms. Carmen didn't speak until Mama finally let go of Bronwyn. "Why didn't you use the tutoring center?"

"Because the computers aren't always available," Bronwyn mumbled. Her excuse sounded pathetic, even to her.

"Promise me and your mother, you'll never be on the streets alone again." Her voice caught, and Bronwyn saw sadness well in her eyes. "I've seen too much."

Bronwyn shifted her weight, feeling stupid for her naivety. Weather had said the same thing. "I promise."

"Let's get you fed." Mama pulled Bronwyn's hand. "I saved you a plate."

Bronwyn followed Mama down the hall, but not before gazing out the window. Would Weather and her friends sleep under the bridge? What would they eat?

Her heart hurt at the cold reality. Even Markus tugged at her sympathy. What kind of person had he been before the streets hardened him?

They were only a bunch of kids.

Chapter Fifteen
November 2012

I took the jar of jalapenos from Bing before she lost count and dumped the entire contents into the blender. We were nervous enough for high school basketball try-outs; we didn't need to add indigestion to the mix.

A flurry of legs and arms blurred in front of me. Maybe trying to make our lucky shakes in the locker room wasn't the greatest idea. Middle school was one thing. High school came with different rules.

I grabbed a handful of paper towels to wipe up the sticky ice cream residue that Bing had dripped all over the bench.

"Almost done?" Teegan laced her shoes. "We have to be on the court in less than five minutes.

I hit the highest speed of the blender and regretted my decision immediately. The lid flew off, drenching me in a bath of milk and soft ice cream. A jalapeno hit me in the nose.

All activity ceased. Every head turned toward me. Heat crept up my neck.

"Nice." Bing's applause broke the silence. For once she wasn't the klutz.

So much for our lucky shakes. This was not the best way to begin try-outs.

Teegan eyed the remainder which sloshed at the bottom of the blender. Our lucky shakes tasted bad enough. We would choke trying to finish this half-mixed batch off.

"Forget it," she hissed. "I'm going to practice." The locker room door slammed behind her.

I felt terrible. Teegan had enough pressure as the coach's daughter. Our spicy milkshake ritual preceded every try-out and every game. I didn't want to be the one jinxing our high school career.

"Let me help you." Hoot tackled the floor with a handful of paper towels while I wiped off the bench. Tabasco sauce splattered my practice shirt.

"Does it look bad?"

Hoot knew better than to lie. "Awful."

I needed a stain stick and more time, but I had neither, so I marched onto the court with all the confidence I could muster. Being late would not help my skills.

Coach Miller frowned at Hoot and me. "Tardies are unacceptable, ladies."

So much for any special attention for being his daughter's best friend.

Teegan mouthed an apology.

I was the one who messed up, but I appreciated her gesture. Time to focus, or I could kiss my chances goodbye.

Coach Miller consulted his clipboard. Seriousness replaced his fun-loving nature. Our history as neighbors didn't matter. Here on the basketball court, he ruled the team as head coach. A handful of varsity players stood on the sidelines, ready to help with drill work. They would no doubt assess the skills of outstanding freshmen who might make their coveted ranks.

I wiped my sweaty palms on my basketball shorts. Teegan tried to steady her breathing. She'd dreamed of playing for her dad's team from the time she could dribble. Hoot gave me a nod, and Bing

190

flashed me a smile. Even though Mia had hurt me, I wished she'd changed her mind. The season—if we made the team—wouldn't be the same without her.

"Let's see what you have." Coach Miller didn't waste time. Forget the easy stuff. He started with a regimen that would've made a soldier cry. I couldn't even think about the season. I'd be lucky if I survived try-outs. No wonder the universities wanted to recruit Teegan's dad to coach their teams. He was that good.

Sweat drenched me by the time we took our first break. I gulped down my water bottle in seconds.

"I'm dying." I wiped a droplet off my lips.

"I'm already dead." Hoot dried the perspiration from her skin with a hand towel.

"Just kill me now." Bing flung herself to the floor.

Only Teegan seemed unaffected. "Come on, girls. Think how much Coach will push us this year."

"That's supposed to inspire us?" I joined Bing on the floor and leaned against the wall. My legs felt like noodles. I wasn't in shape for this.

"We've dreamed of this day since our basketball games at the YMCA." Excitement lit her eyes. "Don't you remember?"

Coach Miller blew his whistle before I could answer. Teegan stuck out her hand to help me up. "Come on. You can do it. Imagine the Maj up in the stands cheering for you."

The second half of practice was equally brutal. If I had half of Teegan's determination, I might've fared better. As it was, I left practice convinced I didn't even make the reserve team. Bing and Hoot felt just as discouraged.

I avoided Coach's eyes when I climbed into the back of his Ranger for a ride home.

"Nice job out there today, girls."

I wanted to tell him he didn't have to be nice, but he seemed to read my mind. "Really." Coach smiled. "I saw a lot of potential out there today."

Teegan poked me in the leg and grinned. "Told you."

I still had my doubts, but his encouragement reminded me of the Maj. He was always rooting for me—win or lose. After a bad loss in elementary school, the Maj took me out for ice cream and let me pick one topping for every point I missed.

The cashier raised an eyebrow when I went to the register, but the Maj just laughed. Gummy worms and sprinkles buried the ice cream. The resulting sugar rush definitely took away my blues.

If only the Maj would be here when the roster got posted. Ice cream piled with toppings wouldn't be enough to counter the bad news. I would need a hug from my dad.

***

I didn't want to look at the single sheet of paper outside Coach Miller's office which sealed my fate, so Teegan told me the news.

My shoulders slumped.

"I knew it," I sighed.

Teegan grabbed my shoulders and repeated the words that didn't register in my brain. "You made the team!"

"What?" My eyes bugged out. "Are you serious?" I almost ripped the roster off the wall to check for myself.

Sure enough. Josie Jameson was on the list, along with Teegan, Bing, and Hoot.

The four of us clasped arms and did a happy dance in the hallway. We made the freshmen girls' team. I couldn't wait to email the Maj. I could almost hear his cheers from halfway across the world.

Five practices later, I sat on the bench, trying to focus on the action on the court. The first game of my high school season was enough to make me nervous. Knowing the Maj wasn't here made concentration difficult. He was due home any day on leave; the anticipation was killing me. Even our lucky shakes hadn't pushed me into game mode. Clinking our cups together without Mia made her absence all the more real.

My dog tags dug into my palms from squeezing too hard. Coach Miller made an exception during practices, but he wouldn't let me wear my dog tags for games. I knew safety was the concern, but how could I explain the ache of not feeling the metal against my heart?

Coach Miller called a time out, and my teammates ran to the sidelines. His calm demeanor contrasted with our hyperactive middle school coach. Her unconventional antics in the classroom spilled onto the court in her high energy and exuberance.

"Nice defense, ladies." He pulled me and Hoot off the bench. "You two are in. I want to see more passing. Watch each other. Show me some of the plays we've been working on in practice."

The whistle blew, and I was in the game. Nervous energy made my heart race. High school ball came with more pressure. Making varsity depended on what happened on the freshman and

JV courts. Talent on the varsity team brought scholarships and offers to play college ball.

I shook my head to clear it. If I didn't focus, I'd make a stupid mistake. My opponent intercepted the ball and took off for the basket. I tore after her and blocked the shot. The crowd cheered, making me smile. If only the Maj were in the stands.

Bing scored a lay-up, and we slapped hands. Two more minutes on the clock, and we lagged behind by six points.

Teegan dribbled down court and passed the ball to me. Coach Miller paced the sidelines. Did I dare try a three-point shot?

Split-second decisions on the court could make or break a game. When the swish of the net brought the crowd to their feet, I pumped my arm in victory. Three more points to even the score before the half.

I exchanged a look with Hoot and Teegan. We didn't have to say a word. The same goal coursed through each of us.

"Let's do this, ladies," I muttered, charging down the court.

We needed to block the next play, but our opponents played the oldest trick in the book— running down the clock. They passed the ball back and forth, taunting us until I wanted to scream. Our efforts fell short when the buzzer sounded, and the half ended with us trailing behind.

"We still got this." Teegan swatted me as we ran toward her dad. "Don't let them win the head game."

She was right. Half the battle was not giving up. Losing by a few points at half-time didn't determine the game.

Coach Miller rallied us around him when the PA system cracked, interrupting his pep talk. "Can I have your attention?" The announcer quieted the crowd. "We have a very special guest joining our game this evening."

I cocked my head, curious about the strange announcement. Coach and the girls stared at the entrance to the gym. Teegan's grin made my hopes soar. I'd read a dozen stories about deployed soldiers surprising their kids. Could the special guest really be my dad?

I craned my neck, and the familiar frame silhouetted by the light stopped my heartbeat.

"All the way from Afghanistan on leave, please join me in welcoming Major Greg Jameson."

I took off running, vaguely aware of the screaming fans who rose to cheer. The metal bleachers reverberated with the roar of stomping feet.

"Dad!" I leapt into the Maj's arms, and he swung me around.

"Surprise." He held me out at arm's length. "Look at you. Playing high school basketball."

My heart thudded in my chest. I was a sweaty mess, but I didn't care. Was I dreaming? I touched his weathered hands, the skin darkened from the sun. Would the mirage disappear, leaving me disappointed?

"It's really me." He read my thoughts. "I'm really here."

I threw my arm around his thick neck again and clung to the Maj for several minutes, afraid to let go. The crowd cheered louder.

The announcer's voice came over the PA system again, breaking my trance. "So what do you think, fans? I hear father and daughter are a little competitive."

195

I broke from our embrace and reddened. All eyes were on the Maj and me.

Coach Miller approached with a jersey. The girls stood near the bench, their arms linked and looking very guilty. Even Mia had joined them from the bleachers.

"You guys had something to do with this, didn't you?" I mouthed.

They nodded with wet eyes. I couldn't be mad, even if I didn't like the attention.

"Welcome home, neighbor." Coach gave the Maj a big hug. "Any words for our audience?"

"It's good to be home." He draped his arm over my shoulder. "I'm going to enjoy every minute of the next two weeks."

Coach turned to me. "So tell the audience a little about the running competition between you two."

The microphone squeaked when he placed it near my lips, making me jump back.

I cleared my throat and tried again. "We make everything a competition—foosball, racing on our ATVs, anything that can be won. When the Maj left, we were tied."

Coach took back the microphone, his eyes twinkling. "So what do you think of a little free throw contest to break that tie?"

I eyed the Maj, and he nodded.

"Hooah!" He yelled out the Army mantra and pumped his fists. "Let's play some ball."

The crowd roared.

**

A wire basket filled with balls stood between the Maj and me. Black PT shorts and basketball jersey

196

replaced his desert BDUs. Tennis shoes squeaked against the court instead of combat boots. Mom waved from the crowd.

"Winner gets double points." The Maj upped the stakes to our competition.

"You sure?" I gritted my teeth. "I've been practicing for months."

"Me, too." He gave a sly smile and got into position. "Our court's just a little more rugged."

The whistle blew, and the Maj took the shot. We each had a minute to score as many free throws as we could.

"Bam!" The Maj exulted in his first basket.

I rolled my eyes.

"What's wrong, Rooster?" He took another shot and scored. "You're not afraid, are you?"

"Hardly," I deadpanned. It was crazy how quickly we got back into our competitive banter, even after only a few minutes together.

Seven baskets later, the whistle signaled his time was up.

"Beat that." The Maj checked me the ball.

My frown made him laugh. "What? I thought you were happy to see the old man?"

Of course I was thrilled to see the Maj. What did happiness have to do with anything? We were in the middle of a cut-throat competition. The rush of the fight cast all other emotions aside.

"Ready?" the referee asked.

I got into position. Someone in the crowd yelled out my name, but I forced out all distractions and stared at the basket.

The trill of the whistle set me in motion. My first ball hit the rim and bounced off. I grabbed another ball and scored. Orange blurred in front of my eyes

197

as I snapped my wrist in free throw after free throw. When the whistle blew, I couldn't believe it. We were tied.

"Seven-seven." The announcer blared from the sound system. "Looks like father and daughter will continue their competition off the court."

The Maj and I slapped hands. "Good job." He swung his arm around me. Applause and catcalls broke around us as we walked off the court. Pride swelled inside me. They were clapping for my dad, my hero.

My feet had wings during the second half of the game. Just knowing the Maj sat in the crowd rooting for me bolstered my game. My eyes met his every time I scored. Coach Miller didn't call a sub for me once, knowing how precious each minute on the court was to both the Maj and me.

When the final buzzer sounded, the girls descended on me. The scoreboard reflected our win, but the numbers barely registered in my mind. My dad rushed onto the court and lifted me off my feet. I was on top of the world.

***

The Maj handed me an elaborately carved wooden box when we got home. "For you."

I traced my fingers along the raised patterns of flowers and geometric patterns.

"Open it." A strange grin lit his face.

I lifted the lid, but nothing happened. "Is the opening on the side?" I turned over the box.

"The key's hidden."

The scalloped design on the front panel had a loose piece of wood, but it didn't open no matter what I tried.

The Maj leaned forward. "Try the base."

Five minutes disappeared before I finally figured out how to shift the box off its base. When it moved, the loose scalloped piece dropped down to reveal a key hole. "Clever." I nodded in appreciation.

"So where's the key?" Curiosity got the better of Mom. She wore a necklace of lapis lazuli the Maj brought home for her. The deep blue gemstone had been mined in northeast Afghanistan.

The Maj shifted the box back in place. "Notice anything else about the base?"

"It's not a single piece of wood." I wiggled the front.

"Push it to the left."

I had to press hard before the panel moved, and a key dropped from a hollowed place in the box.

"Amazing, huh?" The Maj took a sip of his iced tea. "The boxes are popular with the local craftsmen."

I twisted the key and opened the box. The ninth envelope which read "courage" rested on the red velvet lining.

"You took it from the foot locker?"

The Maj nodded as I pulled out an old picture of him in front of a rappel tower. His grin stretched under a helmet that looked too big on his head. A caption on the back read, "Basic Training 1987."

"You know I was afraid of heights," the index card read. "Rappelling made me face my nightmare. Challenge #9: Face something you fear."

I shook my head before he even asked the question. Climbing the old burr oak was one thing.

Anything more, and heights scared me. A bouldering trip with the Maj and Colter resulted in a broken ankle when I lost my foothold and fell several feet down a cliff.

"That was five years ago." The Maj read my mind. "It's time to try again."

I exhaled. Colter jumped out of helicopters at Airborne School. He loved the rush of adrenaline. Me? I preferred the ground.

"You can do it." He patted me on the back. "You and me and Colt this weekend."

I managed a weak smile. Did I really have a choice? Colter would be home for the weekend, and my brother was even more persuasive than the Maj. Who else had gotten me to shave my eyebrows when I was six—the day before my debut as the flower girl in my cousin's wedding?

Mom was still furious.

Maybe rappelling wouldn't be so bad after all.

***

Sweat beaded Bronwyn's forehead. Fire ignited her skin. She pulled off the blanket and immediately started to shake. The pounding inside her head made her dizzy when she tried to sit up. Bronwyn fell back on her pillow and squeezed her eyes shut, but sleep wouldn't come. She felt too sick.

Bronwyn wished she could make some hot tea and sprawl in front of the TV. She longed to linger in the shower, the cool water beating down on her feverish flesh. But the mission wasn't home.

Mama touched her forehead. "You're burning up." Concern filled her eyes.

Bronwyn tried to answer, but the swelling in her throat made speech difficult.

"You need to see a doctor."

Bronwyn shook her head. They didn't have health insurance. A visit to the doctor was out of the question.

"No arguments." Mama read Bronwyn's mind. "Ms. Carmen told me about a low income clinic a few blocks from here."

A tear slid down Bronwyn's cheek. If only she hadn't walked home from the library in damp clothes. She hated to burden Mama, but she was too weak to protest.

Trudging to the bus stop took all Bronwyn's strength. She dozed in the waiting room while Mama read a magazine and Kenzie played with the toys in the corner. Thoughts of her friends played through her dreams.

Two hours later, they returned from the health clinic with a diagnosis of a sinus infection and orders to rest. Was rest even possible living at the mission?

"I've been where you are." Ms. Carmen's voice got husky when they met her in the hallway. "My girls weren't much older than yours when we found ourselves on the streets. It will get better."

Bronwyn pressed her fingertips to her temples. She wanted to believe Ms. Carmen, but the throbbing in her head demanded her attention. She followed Mama down the hallway and collapsed on the bed.

Despite the light streaming in through the broken blinds, Bronwyn's eyes got weighty. She floated between sleep and wakefulness as Mama rubbed her back and hummed a lullaby she'd almost forgotten.

The song took Bronwyn back to the summer after they'd first fled from her father. They begged tourists for food during

201

the day and slept on the beach at night, the waves rolling in the background as Mama sang her girls to sleep.

Bronwyn had been so scared. Everywhere she looked, his face shadowed her days and haunted her dreams. What would he do when they found them?

The thought made her cry out.

"Hush." Mama squeezed her hand. "Go to sleep. You're safe."

Bronwyn hugged her pillow. She wanted to believe Mama. But they were never safe—even in the big city which seemed to swallow them in anonymity.

The clock was ticking. It was only a matter of time until he found them.

Chapter Sixteen

I strapped on my helmet and tried to steady my breathing. The seat harness pulled at my jeans, pinching my legs. The Maj had gotten permission for us to use the National Guard training grounds, but looking over the five story building made my stomach revolt. Colter wasn't even breaking a sweat.

"I can't do this."

"Yes, you can." Muscles bulged under my brother's Under Armour shirt. He'd bulked up even more since high school, and he was strong then. It was good to have him home—even if it was only for the weekend.

Doubt sent a shiver down my spine. The wind hadn't been noticeable at ground level, but I had to brace myself this high up.

"I'll coach you the whole way down." Colter checked my harness to make sure it was tight and then hooked up the ropes. Normally he'd be taunting me, but his sensitive side won over, and he joined the Maj in encouraging me.

"I believe in you, Rooster." The Maj yelled from below.

My knees knocked together as I tried to gulp down my fear. If the Maj could face battle every day, I could rappel off a building.

"Going over the edge is the hardest." Colter gave me final instructions as he double checked the carabineer. "Ready to do this?"

I wanted to hurl. Sweat beaded my forehead.

"Just do it." My brother sounded like a commercial. "The longer you think about it, the harder it is."

He was right. Standing up here was making me sick. I straddled the edge and resisted the urge to look down. Imagining myself splattered on the ground below would not help my fears.

"Looking good," the Maj encouraged me from below.

His praise fueled my courage. I could do this.

"On rappel," Colter shouted to the Maj.

"On belay," he volleyed back.

"Focus on me," Colter coached me, and the commanding tone in his voice eased my nerves.

I stared into Colter's face framed by a short military buzz. Steely resolve shone from his pale blue eyes. When had my brother turned into a man?

"One. . ." he barked.

I exhaled.

"Two. . ."

I clutched the rappel rope.

"Three. . ."

I inhaled and let go, sure I would plummet to my death. But the rope caught, and my heart bounced back from my throat. Colter was right. The worst was stepping off the edge.

"Perfect." My brother smiled over the top of the building. "That wasn't too bad, was it?"

I managed a smile.

"Now release your hold and walk down the side of the building."

Nothing happened.

"Let out the slack."

I slid too far on my next attempt.

"Remember to brake," Colter commanded. "Pace yourself."

I adjusted my hold until I figured out how to balance the tension.

"You're a regular Spider-Man." The Maj yelled up to me, and I could hear the pride in his voice.

Bouncing against the brick wall was fun. When I touched ground, the Maj grabbed me in a fierce hug.

"Nice job." His rugged smell filled my nostrils.

"Way to go," Colter cheered from the roof. "You did it, sis."

My legs were shaky, but the rush was addicting. "Can I go again?"

The Maj's throaty laugh made me beam. "Definitely." He slapped me on the back.

I headed for the stairs.

"Hey, Rooster," the Maj called out before I disappeared. "I'm proud of you."

Warmth coated my insides. "The Army may have a new recruit," the Maj yelled up to my brother. "The girl is hooked."

***

The digital clock in the Maj's pickup taunted me as we bounced along the gravel road the next afternoon. Every turn of the numbers meant one less minute with my dad and brother. Even though we'd packed a lot into the weekend, I wasn't ready to say goodbye. Colter left in four hours; the Maj left in four days.

I stared out the window, refusing to watch another minute pass. A mobile home nestled in a grove of trees came into view around the next hill.

"That's it," Colt announced.

The Maj parked, and we piled out of the pickup dressed in enough camo, we blended in with the surrounding woods. I grabbed the paintball guns from the back seat and tossed them to the guys.

A friend of Colter's met us at the door. His paintball business was more of a hobby, but his great location was getting popular with all the local paintball junkies.

"Thanks for letting us come out today." Colter gave Rod a bro hug.

"Anytime. It's the least I could do." He shook the Maj's hand. "Thanks for serving our country."

We followed Rod to a break in the trees, and he explained the boundaries and layout of the terrain. A rainbow of paint color smattered tree trunks and brush. His groups were usually larger than our trio, but he'd given us free rein for an hour.

"Obviously, goggles are required, so don't remove your face mask unless you're in the dead zone." He pointed to a marked off area away from the field. "Any questions?"

When we shook our heads, Rod left us to enjoy pelting each other with paint.

Colter checked his gun. "Every man for himself? Winner has the least hits."

"Hooah!" the Maj roared.

A rush of adrenaline coursed through me. I hadn't played paintball since Colter left for basic training, but holding the gun felt as natural as riding the ATVs. I loaded the hopper with neon green paintballs and tightened the strap on my face mask.

Colter raised a battle cry, and we fanned out into the woods like a small platoon of soldiers. Competition was fierce in the Jameson household. I spotted a tree with low hanging branches that would provide great cover. Colter whistled, signaling our war.

My heart thumped against my chest. The Maj peered over a dead tree trunk. I centered him in the crosshairs and fired my first shot. The paintball pinged off his helmet. Score.

The Maj returned fire, but I ducked behind my tree. Paintballs exploded around me.

I blasted the next round at Colter.

"Cover me!" He yelled, then zigzagged toward me like some half-crazed ninja. Out of the corner of my eye, I saw the Maj aim for me.

Realization hit. The two of them had formed a secret alliance.

"What?!" I braced my weapon like a machine gun and sprayed ammo between the two of them. "No fair."

"All's fair in love and war!" Colter took a flying leap toward me, but I twisted out of the way and aimed for his butt.

"Then take this." I hit my target square in the cheeks. Ba'bam. I'd learned from the best—my brother.

"Ouch!" Colter's yelp echoed through the woods. "That's gonna leave a welt."

I laughed as I took off running. The Maj and Colter crashed through the brush behind me. A paintball whizzed past my ear. I wasn't going down.

A dry creek bed loomed ahead. I scanned the terrain, looking for an opening. If I could jump into the ditch and take cover, I could blast them from below. I put on a surge of speed and slid down the embankment. A dead tree which had fallen across the creek bed was the perfect cover. I scurried under its shelter and poked my barrel through an opening in the branches.

They stopped a few feet above me and crouched low, looking for me. I aimed and surprised them with a shower of paint. My spot was perfect. They returned fire, but not one drop touched me.

"You win," Colter called out. "I'm out of paintballs."

I emerged from my cover, ready to gloat, but I should have known better. I walked right into their ambush. The two blasted me until their hoppers emptied.

"Cheaters!" My frown turned to a grin. It was hard to be mad when I felt like a modern art piece getting doused with paint.

"Technically, your brother never said truce." The Maj raised my arm in victory. "You played well. Congratulations, Rooster."

"Nice job, sis." Colter slapped my back and flashed me his famous crooked grin. "I know a couple recruiters who might start calling you."

I snapped a selfie. Paint smudged our faces. The picture would go on my mirror, next to the others of my two heroes.

We trudged back to the truck, laughing about our battle. I wanted the minutes to stretch out as long as possible, but Colter had a plane to board. If only I could hide out in his rucksack.

Mom was waiting at home with a fresh batch of chocolate chip cookies and clean laundry. She didn't cry when Colter left, but I knew the tears would come later in the quiet of the night.

I disappeared into my room and stripped off my paint-splattered camouflage. I already dreaded the next goodbye. Why did the Maj have to go back to Afghanistan?

Four long months loomed ahead of me.

I ripped the calendar off my wall. I couldn't do this one more day.

I tore the paper like a crazy person, ripping each month into tiny pieces. Tears blinded me, but I didn't stop until every day was obliterated.

The Maj was headed back into a war zone.

And there was nothing I could do. My helplessness mocked me.

I just wanted my dad home.

For good.

***

Saying goodbye left me numb for days. If it wasn't for Teegan's family, I would've skipped Thanksgiving while my mom buried herself in work at the hospital.

Teegan dragged me to her house where Savanah leapt into my arms and moved her hands in a blur of motion. "Happy Turkey Day."

When I didn't smile, Savanah took my hand in hers and formed the sign for "turkey."

I tried not to cry. The aroma of homemade pie and turkey reminded me of the Maj's absence.

"Come on." Teegan swung an arm around my neck. "You can't be alone on Thanksgiving. And you're saving me from all the little monsters. My oldest cousin is only ten."

As if on cue, a loud roar rose from the basement. "Speaking of the rug rats." Teegan gritted her teeth. "They're downstairs."

I followed her to the kitchen where the adults had gathered. Teegan introduced me to three aunts who I recognized from family pictures. They echoed their greetings as they busied themselves with last minute preparations.

One of the uncles talked with Teegan's dad as he stood at the island carving the turkey. He wore an apron that read, "Don't mess with the cook."

Christopher, dressed as Batman, and cousin Sam wearing a Superman cape swept into the kitchen and each snagged a piece of meat.

"Hey." His dad waved the carving fork in the air. "Don't touch my turkey."

This only encouraged the superheroes who circled the island a second time. Teegan's mom skirted Sam as she carried the mashed potatoes toward the dining room, but collided with Christopher. The mashed potatoes landed in a lump on the floor.

"Uh, oh," Sam uttered as a hush fell over the room.

Batman cowered in fear. Mashed potatoes were a family favorite.

Savanah, unaware of the silence, broke it when she took a finger and swiped it through the potatoes. "Yum."

"Why not?" Teegan's mom grabbed a serving spoon. "Anyone want to help me scoop off the top?"

One of her sisters dropped to the floor to help. "This is the stuff of legends." She grinned. "The great potato disaster is only going to get better every year we retell the story."

The talk at dinner alternated between sharing blessings and recounting other crazy holiday fiascos. The best was the flying turkey and the cat.

Apparently Sam's mom missed the roaster last year. The raw bird went sliding across the kitchen floor and spooked the cat who knocked into the table. The gravy boat tipped over and got stuck on Fluffy's head. The blind cat darted around the room, screeching in terror.

Things got awkward when it was my turn to share a blessing.

"Has your dad ever gotten shot or been in an explosion?" Sam's question was innocent enough, but all conversation came to a crashing halt.

"Sam!" his dad scolded. "War isn't a superhero movie. Her dad's in danger every day. You need to apologize to Teegan."

He bit his lip, reddening. The kid looked like he could burst into tears.

"It's okay," I regained my composure. "The Maj is safe. He's eating turkey today, too."

Mom's arrival took the edge off the moment. She hadn't bothered to change out of her uniform and looked exhausted, but the enthusiastic greeting from everyone made her face relax. The adults shifted to make room for her, and I kissed her cheek then disappeared downstairs with Teegan.

I fell on the couch in the basement in a food coma. Teegan snapped the waistband of her sweats. "That's why I chose elastic." She eyed me closer. "Sorry about my cousin."

I brushed aside her concern. "He's just a kid. It happens."

Teegan surfed the channels, and I grabbed a blanket. I wouldn't last through a movie.

211

A Nerf dart flew across the room and hit me in the arm, making me jump.

"Christopher," Teegan growled. "You woke up Rooster."

I wiped my eyes. "Did I fall asleep?"

A shadow moved near the foosball table. Sam cocked his gun, and a shower of darts rained over us. Sam followed with another round. Apparently pelting us with Nerf darts was Sam's way of apologizing.

More little bodies appeared, and the battle turned into a crazy free-for-all. Arms flailed, Nerf guns flashed, and darts flew everywhere.

When we finally called a truce, my heart raced from trying out my ninja moves on the cousins. Sam surprised me when he threw his arms around me, his cape still tied around his neck. "I want to be a real superhero like your dad when I get bigger."

I almost cried.

***

Bronwyn knew she should be grateful, but she just wanted to be in their own home. Not eating another communal dinner with a bunch of strangers.

She trudged behind Mama and Kenzie at the end of the long line for Thanksgiving dinner.

"You okay?" Mama touched her forehead. "You're not getting sick again, are you?"

"Just tired." Bronwyn managed a smile.

"Ms. Carmen gave me a list of apartments to check out." Mama lit up. "Want to go looking this weekend?"

Kenzie clapped her hands and cheered.

212

The news couldn't have been better, but Bronwyn choked on her answer. Oliver stared at her from the other side of the line. He was volunteering.

Shock rendered them both speechless.

"Turkey?" he finally regained his composure.

Bronwyn wanted to run, but where could she go? Oliver had discovered her awful secret.

He gave his tongs to another volunteer and cornered her before she could follow Mama and Kenzie to a table. "Why didn't you tell me?"

Tears burned Bronwyn's eyes.

"Sorry. Dumb question." Oliver got flustered. Compassion filled his face. "I wouldn't want anyone to know I was homeless either."

Bronwyn held back the tears and stared at her feet.

"I like you." Oliver grabbed her hand. "Nothing changes that."

Bronwyn blinked, not sure she'd heard right.

"Will you go to the winter dance with me?" Oliver looked like he would drop to his knee if the place wasn't so crowded. "I don't care if you dress in rags. You'll still be the prettiest girl there."

Before Bronwyn could answer, someone bumped into her. She lost her balance and fell into Oliver's arms. An electric jolt sent shock waves through her body.

Bronwyn gasped. For the briefest moment, the world stood still as she looked into his eyes. Bronwyn knew she could trust Oliver.

"Is that a yes?" He was the first to find his voice.

Bronwyn nodded. She couldn't turn Oliver down again. Homecoming nearly killed her.

Oliver let out a whoop. "She said yes!"

A few heads turned, making Bronwyn laugh.

213

"Said yes to what?" Ms. Carmen walked by them. Bronwyn reddened.

"The winter dance with me," Oliver boasted.

"That's wonderful." Ms. Carmen clasped her hands. "And I have just the surprise."

Oliver wanted to meet Mama and Kenzie, so after the crowd cleared, Ms. Carmen took Bronwyn and Kenzie to the back of Hope's House while Mama and Oliver helped with cleanup.

They stopped in front of a door Bronwyn had always assumed was a cleaning supply closet. Ms. Carmen fished a set of keys from her pocket.

Kenzie glowed with anticipation. "What's inside?"

Ms. Carmen turned the key and pushed open the door. "Dresses."

Bronwyn's jaw dropped. Rows of dress racks met her sight. A rainbow of colors and sequin and ruffles filled the room. Mia would be hyperventilating—shocked into a fashion coma.

Kenzie squealed. "It's like a closet for a princess."

"One of these should work for your dance." Ms. Carmen pocketed her keys. "Take your pick."

Bronwyn didn't know what to say.

Kenzie darted behind the closest rack. Her sister would get lost among the fabrics and colors playing dress up.

"I'm sorry I didn't say something earlier." Ms. Carmen smoothed out a dress. "I get so busy, I forgot about Homecoming."

Bronwyn reached a tentative finger toward a red gown as if touching the material would make it disappear. "Where did you get all these dresses?"

"People donate formal dresses all year round for our annual fundraiser in February."

214

Bronwyn pinched her flesh, sure she was dreaming.

"I'm going to help with cleanup." Ms. Carmen headed down the hall. "I'll check back after I'm done."

Bronwyn ran her hand along a deep blue gown with spaghetti straps, the satin cool against her fingertips. Her heart leapt. Before they fled, Nana had taught her basic stitching on an old Singer sewing machine, encouraging Bronwyn to dream about designing clothes and opening a boutique someday.

"Help," Kenzie's muffled voice broke her thoughts.

She peered around the rack and laughed. Two arms stuck in the air as her sister wiggled inside an unzipped dress.

Bronwyn pulled the hot pink material over Kenzie's face, and chestnut hair sprang from her head with the static electricity.

"Do I look pretty?" Kenzie twirled in a circle.

"Fancy." Bronwyn smiled, wishing the room had a floor-length mirror for her sister.

Her sister bounced down the aisle until a beaded purple dress stopped her. "Ooh. How pretty."

Bronwyn couldn't help but smile at her sister's excitement. She wandered among the racks looking for something less elaborate. Bronwyn didn't want to stick out. Not when she had spent almost five years now trying to become invisible so her father wouldn't find them.

A black dress with a sweetheart neckline caught her attention. Bronwyn pulled it from the rack and turned the hanger to examine the front and back. Simple, yet elegant. If only her friends were here to help her choose.

"Look at me." Kenzie spun in front of her, a blur of purple.

"Wow." Bronwyn caught her sister before she fell over from dizziness.

215

Kenzie scrunched her nose at Bronwyn's choice. "Black is boring."

"Maybe for you." Bronwyn poked her sister, and Kenzie giggled. "But I happen to like the color."

Bronwyn took off her hoodie and pulled the dress over her tank top. "What do you think now?"

Kenzie cocked her head. "It needs ruffles and beads."

Bronwyn smiled at her little critic and smoothed the dress with her hand. Even without a mirror, she knew the dress was the one.

"Beautiful." Mama appeared in the doorway. "That will be perfect for the dance."

Bronwyn blushed. "Really?"

Kenzie bounced between them before she could answer. "Do I look like a princess, Mama?"

"Like Cinderella." Mama hugged Kenzie.

Bronwyn knew why her sister wanted to twirl around the room. The same urge welled inside her, but she felt silly.

Mama squeezed Bronwyn's hand. "Kenzie's not the only princess in the room."

She couldn't help but smile. Bronwyn felt like royalty.

Chapter Seventeen
December 2012

When my grandparents got sick and had to cancel their trip to see us over Christmas, I wanted to skip the whole holiday season.

Pouting got old after a day, though, so I thought about the Maj's last challenge—the one I'd found with the Christmas decorations. "The holidays can be tough during deployment, but don't forget to enjoy the season. Challenge #10: Let life consume you. Do something for someone else. Passion ignited sets you on fire."

Maybe Mom and I could volunteer at the homeless shelter.

She didn't need much convincing since neither of us could bear the thought of celebrating Christmas alone. I called the volunteer coordinator and found out they needed help wrapping gifts for the kids at the shelter.

On a last minute whim, I stuck a Santa hat on my flat daddy and loaded him into Mom's hybrid. The Maj's cardboard clone could serve alongside us, and maybe even bring a few smiles to people fighting their own private battles of survival.

We drove through snowy streets past buildings laced in white lights and parked next to the shelter. A lady at the front desk directed us past an artificial tree decorated with loops of construction paper and kids' artwork toward a room where the other volunteers had gathered.

"Rooster?" the familiar voice reached my ears.

I turned to see Jada. Was she back at the shelter?

"Are you volunteering, too?" She introduced me to her mother.

Of course Jada's mom didn't remember me from the Cardboard City audience, but she knew my mom because of the situation with her son.

"How are you doing?" Mom handled what could've been awkward exactly like she cared for her patients—with dignity. "I've thought of you several times since Jason's funeral."

"Thank you." Alison's eyes betrayed her sadness. "That's why we're here volunteering." Her gaze drifted across the room. "The shelter helped us so much last year. We want to pay it forward this Christmas."

"Good for you." Mom squeezed her hand. "You look great, too."

"Thanks." She blushed at the compliment. "My daughter and I are training for our first half marathon to raise awareness of veterans suffering from PTSD."

"Really?" Mom's eyebrows lifted. "I might have to join you to keep up with my husband. He's been logging in the miles on his deployment."

Jada pointed to my flat daddy. "Your dad?"

I stood him up. "He loves Christmas, so I thought it'd be fun to bring him."

I wondered if she ever got a flat daddy of her brother, but she changed the subject. "Come look at the gifts. The kids are going to be so excited."

The utility room was packed with everything from dolls to footballs to board games. Two ladies sorted gifts by age groups while an older man set out wrapping paper and bows. Seeing all the toys made my own heart flip flop. I was so glad we'd get to be a small part of making Christmas special for kids at the shelter.

"Who's your friend?" a bald guy with a huge grin asked Jada.

"Hi, Henry." Jada had the same confidence I saw at camp. She'd cut her bangs, and her hair was in a cute bun. "This is Josie."

Henry shook my hand. "Thanks for coming to help. We need all the extra hands we can get."

Our moms walked into the room, and Henry called all the volunteers together to give us instructions. I felt like one of Santa's elves.

Jada and I had wrapping paper duty which proved to be quite entertaining. My first attempt at wrapping a soccer ball made us both bust out laughing.

"Need some wrapping paper with that tape?" Jada pushed down a stray piece.

I turned over my pathetic wrapping job and slapped on a big blue bow. At least I chose some fun paper. Snoopy and Woodstock would make any kid smile. I handed the gift to a volunteer in charge of tagging the packages.

My mom and Alison hit it off. The two didn't stop talking as they wrapped gifts together. Coming to the shelter had been a good thing. Focusing on someone else was way better than wallowing in our own hurt.

I grabbed a board game next. *Operation* had been a favorite with me and the Maj when I was a kid.

"Wanna play?" I asked my flat daddy, and I swear the Maj winked. I almost dropped my tube of wrapping paper.

Jada stopped mid-tape and grinned. "You okay?"

I decided not to tell her about my little hallucination. "Just clumsy."

Soon we were all out of gifts. Jada massaged her wrist as we stared at the stack which rose to the ceiling.

"That's a lot of presents."

Imagining the kids opening the toys made me feel like I'd opened a huge gift myself. What had the Maj said about passion and letting life consume you?

Mom surprised me when she suggested ice skating—one of our family Christmas traditions. We'd decided not to go without the Maj, but I was glad she changed her mind and invited Jada and her mother.

Jada had never skated before, so she wobbled on the ice.

"Hug the wall." I caught her. "And don't try that." I pointed to a pair in the center of the rink with obvious training. They made me dizzy with the circles they spun.

"They make it look so easy." Jada made her first lap around the ice.

"You're doing good." I gave up trying to skate backwards. Without the Maj, I was too slow.

We waved to our moms who were huddled in a warming tent drinking coffee. My flat daddy sat between them. "Ready to let go of the wall?"

Jada proved to be a fast learner. By the time the Zamboni came out to freshen the ice, she even added some speed.

"Someone's having fun." We trekked toward the concessions stand for hot chocolate.

Jada rubbed the top of her legs with her gloves. "I'm going to be sore tomorrow, but I can't wait to skate again."

Alison moved over to let us warm in front of the heat which blew out of a large duct. The rush of air was loud, but felt good.

Christmas lights twinkled as the sky darkened, lighting the rink and making the ice sparkle.

"It looks magical." Jada stood on her skates. "Want to skate some more?"

I didn't want to leave my cocoon of warmth, but I couldn't say no when Jada's eyes lit up like a little kid.

The skating direction had changed, so we merged into the traffic of skaters. Jada didn't even look like a first time skater. With some practice, she would pass my skill level.

"You're a natural."

Her cheeks glowed. "I could stay out here all night."

I puffed out smoke. The temperature had dropped since we'd arrived. "How about 15 more minutes? I'm losing feeling in my fingers."

I felt like a human icicle by the time we left, but Jada didn't seem to notice the cold. She couldn't wait to ice skate again.

We passed a woman bundled up in layers sitting in a doorstop, and Jada's chatter stopped. I couldn't imagine being homeless on such a cold night.

"You okay?" I asked, hugging my flat daddy close.

Jada sighed. "Just remembering."

I had no idea what to say. Being cold and hungry had to be awful. My one night in Cardboard City didn't even compare.

When we arrived at Mom's hybrid, I wasn't surprised when she invited Jada and Alison to Christmas dinner. "It won't be anything fancy," she apologized. "Josie and I didn't feel like doing a traditional feast."

"It sounds perfect." Jada's mom smiled. "Thanks."

Jada surprised me with a hug. "Today was fun."

"Yeah." I smiled, stuffing my flat daddy into the back seat. "Definitely better than being home alone."

***

Bronwyn wanted to call the girls and tell them all the details about the winter dance. The entire night had felt like a dream—the sparkle of the lights that transformed the school gymnasium, the way Oliver looked at her when she entered the room, and the feel of his arms around her when they danced.

Instead, she held the wrist corsage which Oliver had given her, grateful Ms. Carmen had agreed to dry the flowers in her office until moving day.

"Excited?" Mama sat forward on the bus seat and clutched her lone bag. Kenzie looked like she could do cartwheels down the aisle.

"Very." Bronwyn grinned. Mama had signed the leasing agreement yesterday after work. No more living at the mission. They finally had their own apartment.

The sound of the air brakes signaled their new stop. Mama practically jumped off the bus. Bronwyn and Kenzie hurried down the steps behind her.

The apartment complex rose before them like a castle. The keys in Mama's hand clinked together, ringing like the sound of freedom.

They trekked up a flight of stairs and headed to the end of the hallway. The girls held hands as Mama turned the knob to their new home. Bronwyn wanted to kiss the ground.

The apartment wasn't fancy—two bedrooms, a bathroom, living room, and kitchen—but it was their little corner in the universe, and it was furnished. Bronwyn took a sharp breath and inhaled the smell of freshly cleaned carpet. She peeled off her socks and savored the feel of the soft fibers between her bare toes.

Bronwyn's gaze fell on the small table next to the couch. A candle stood next to a bottle of bubbly grape juice and three plastic glasses.

"What's all this?" Mama picked up a card from Ms. Carmen which was propped against the juice. "Welcome home."

"How thoughtful." Tears welled in Mama's eyes. "She must've talked to the manager and snuck the gifts inside while I was at work."

Kenzie disappeared into the bedroom and came out squealing. She clutched a doll that looked like Abigail. Disbelief filled her face. "For me?"

Bronwyn felt her heart swell inside her chest. Ms. Carmen had never shamed them for being homeless, and her kindness made her want to live the same way.

"There's something for you, too." Kenzie tugged on Bronwyn, pulling her to the room.

She narrowed her eyes. "Really?"

A basketball rested on top of the second twin bed. Bronwyn cradled the ball in her arms, and breathed the familiar rubbery smell into her lungs. She was back on the court with Teegan, Rooster, Bing, Hoot, and Mia. How did Ms. Carmen know?

For a full minute, Mama and her girls stood in the living room breathing in the quiet. Bronwyn exhaled slowly as if the slightest movement would pop the bubble. What had the old homeless man told Kenzie? Fairy tales were dead.

Not today.

They wandered from room to room, touching the walls and eyeing one another in awe. Were the days of waiting in line for a bed really over? Were the nights of sleeping in a room full of strangers a distant memory?

In Mama's bedroom, Kenzie was the first to plop down backward on the bed. Mama and Bronwyn followed, their hair fanning out on the bedspread in a montage of browns.

"Pinch me." Mama held out her arms. "I think I'm dreaming."

Kenzie's poke made Mama laugh. "Someone's looking for a tickle war." She pinned Kenzie while Bronwyn tickled her sister.

Kenzie's giggles filled the apartment. Bronwyn grinned. For the first time in months, she finally felt at home.

Chapter Eighteen
January/February 2013

High school basketball consumed January and February. A good thing. Otherwise I would've gone crazy counting down the final days before the Maj returned.

We'd only lost two games, so Coach Miller pushed us hard. He saw potential in his freshmen, and he wanted us to gel as a team before we made varsity.

Our middle school coach made an appearance the night we went into overtime. I could hear her cheers over the rest of the fans. Like always, she stood out in her kaleidoscope of colored attire, shouting out pointers like a back seat driver. She was lucky the refs didn't kick her out of the game.

Teegan cemented our victory with a last second basket. The home crowd went wild. Coach was the first to congratulate us.

"Nice defense, ladies." She hugged each of her former players. "Where's Mia? Didn't she make the team?"

"Over here." She hopped down from the bleachers. "I joined the color guard instead."

If Coach was disappointed, she didn't show it. "Good for you." She hugged Mia then turned to my flat daddy. His cardboard presence made every game. "Think your dad will make it home to see you play?"

I told her about his surprise appearance a few weeks before Thanksgiving. "We're down to the final month. The team replacing his unit is already on Afghan soil."

Coach beamed. "That's wonderful news, Rooster. I know it's been a long year."

Mom joined us on the gym floor. As she and Coach talked, the girls and I made plans to hang out at Bing's house and order pizza.

Mia looked reluctant until Teegan broke the ice. "You have to come. We—I—miss you."

"Ahh." Bing slung one arm around Teegan and the other around Mia. "I knew you two couldn't stay mad at each other forever."

Mia broke into a huge smile. "I've missed you guys, too." She eyed me. "I'm sorry for betraying you."

The girls didn't know about Symone and Grace finding out about the geocache hunt, and I didn't say anything. I'd made my share of mistakes with my friends. The past was past.

Bing pulled Hoot and me into their circle, and we locked arms. As the tension disappeared between us, I couldn't help but wish Bronwyn were here.

Mom's phone rang, killing our Hallmark moment. The color drained from her face. A deep foreboding made my insides go cold. Something bad had happened.

"There's been an attack," her voice trembled.

My knees locked, making my vision blur. I would have fallen if the girls hadn't caught me. "What . . . what happened?" The question tasted like poison.

"A convoy of military trucks got ambushed." Mom steadied herself against Coach. "Three soldiers from the unit are in the hospital. One is in critical condition."

Dry heaves rose to my throat. Was the Maj hurt? How about Harrison? More faces flashed across my mind.

226

"The sergeant major is fighting for his life," Mom stumbled over her words. "He's en route to an American military hospital in Germany. Harrison was in a Humvee with the convoy, but he escaped injury."

Waves of disbelief and confusion rolled over me. I fought the urge to panic. "And the Maj?"

"Safe." Mom breathed a sigh of relief.

I could've kissed the ground, but I didn't trust my jelly legs. Bing didn't hold back, though. She leapt across the floor, performing her own crazy victory dance in my place.

Mia just shook her head. "Sorry, Rooster. The girl has no shame."

Leave it to Bing to lighten the toughest of situations. My heart rate finally slowed.

"The Maj is alive." Bing grabbed my hands. "He's S-A-F-E." She tried to pull me into her dance, but I shook my head. The sergeant major was still in critical condition.

Bing tried to persuade me with a pouty lip, but I didn't budge. When the Maj stood in front of me—eyeball to eyeball on American soil—then I would celebrate. I'd dance my heart out.

***

I wanted to throw a shoe at the computer. The screen froze again in the middle of our Skype session with the Maj. The stress levels were high enough from the attack. Everyone was on edge. Mom had been on the phone for hours with the other soldiers' families since we got the news. If only we could connect once with the Maj without getting broken up.

227

My sour mood only worsened when I stared at my pile of homework. Why did teachers assume weekends gave them permission to double our work?

I fell back on my bed and closed my eyes. I should be grateful the Maj was safe. But I'd been a wreck since the attack.

Porter, the sergeant major who was in critical condition, had a wife and two young kids. Pictures on Facebook showed a little boy with missing teeth and a toddler holding a favorite stuffed elephant. Porter's wife didn't look much older than Katrina. He was too young to die.

Fear and worry knotted my insides. I had to get out of the house or I'd explode.

I grabbed the February envelope marked "anyway" and found myself in front of the burr oak in the yard between Teegan's house and mine.

"Seriously?" I muttered out loud. The cache had been in front of me for months, and I'd never noticed.

I scaled the branches, just imagining the Maj climbing into the heart of the tree to plant the clue. I sat in my favorite nook and hugged my knees. A hundred *what ifs* filled my mind.

What if the Maj came home missing a leg? What if he could never climb a tree again? What if the Maj lost his sight? What about a brain injury?

Crooked limbs twisted around me like the questions tangled in a knot in my head. Death had overshadowed all my other fears. But what if life never returned to normal when the Maj came home? What if an injury changed everything?

Memories of the Maj and me played in front of me like a silent movie. Camping together.

Geocaching. Riding the trails on our ATVs. Paintball battles. Kayaking on the lake. Snowboarding.

Tears welled in my eyes. What if our adventures together were over?

Heaviness settled over me. The cold seeped through my hoodie and numbed my flesh. I had a geocache to find, but I didn't care.

I sat among the branches until the sun touched the horizon and colored the sky. My gaze fell on Colter's carving. The Maj had wedged a small box wrapped in duct tape above my initials. The camouflage pattern had disguised the cache for months. Several strips of paper rested inside the box like fortunes in a cookie.

Even if you're afraid, be brave anyway.

When you feel weak, be strong anyway.

When you feel like giving up, try anyway.

When you're hurting, love anyway.

Even if I don't come home, live anyway.

My fingers trembled as I read the last strip of paper. The Maj was inspired by *The Paradoxical Commandments* originally penned by Dr. Kent Keith and hung on the wall of Mother Teresa's children's home in Calcutta, India.

Sobs shook my body until the tears finally stopped. Darkness shrouded me when I finally climbed down from the tree.

I didn't feel brave or strong or tough. I just wanted my dad to come home.

***

Bronwyn dribbled the basketball in the gym while Mr. Reuben mopped the hall outside the court. The custodian didn't care if she practiced free throw shots after school while Mama worked on lesson plans. She'd gotten a teaching job at Kenzie's school after another teacher quit midyear because of health reasons.

The thud of the ball matched her pulse. Bronwyn fell into the zone where everything except the orange ball faded to black. Swish. She grabbed the rebound and took off down the court. She could run back and forth between the nets all night. The girls felt somehow closer here on the court with her.

"Ready to head home?" Mama stood in the doorway dressed in a long skirt and fitted black blouse. Kenzie chomped on an apple beside her.

They piled into the used Chevy Malibu Mama bought a week earlier and headed to their apartment. Bronwyn leaned back against the seat. Things were finally looking up.

"Ms. Carmen's coming to supper," Mama reminded her. "Can I drop you off at the store for a few things while Kenzie and I start the lasagna?"

Bronwyn took the list Mama offered. The store on the corner was across the street from the apartment complex, so she finished shopping in no time and headed out the door.

A black BMW made Bronwyn's knees buckle.

He was here. At the apartments.

Ms. Carmen pulled into the lot seconds later and rolled down her window. "What's wrong, Bronwyn? You look like you've seen a ghost."

"He's here," she rushed. "Call 911."

Bronwyn didn't wait for Ms. Carmen to park. She bolted up the steps and burst through the apartment door. Her father spun around and glared at her with demonic eyes. A knife glinted in the light. Blood trickled from a cut on Mama's cheek. He'd broken his own rule. He never touched her face.

"Shut up!" he screamed. Kenzie whimpered in the corner clutching her new doll, the one she named Annalise. "Silence."

Fear pinched Bronwyn's throat. How had he found them?

"You're done running." He pushed Mama against the table, every strand of his flawless hair in perfect place. "I want you back."

A siren screamed outside. He grasped the knife and pointed at Bronwyn. "Did you call the cops?"

She backed against the wall, terrified.

"Put down the knife." Two cops fanned into the apartment, guns raised. Her father cursed, but didn't put up a fight. Handcuffs contrasted with his tailored pants and impeccably pressed cotton shirt.

Bronwyn collapsed into Ms. Carmen when she stepped into the room. "It's going to be okay," she murmured. "The nightmare is over."

The cops pushed him into the hall. "You'll hear from my lawyer." His threats died down the stairs.

Mama cradled Kenzie and rocked back and forth. Mascara ran down her cheeks.

Tears burned Bronwyn's eyes. "How'd he find us?"

"The Corolla," Mama's voice trembled. "His private investigator traced the vehicle identification number."

Kenzie peered into Mama's eyes. "Why did the bad man hurt you?"

Bronwyn and Mama exchanged a glance. Kenzie didn't know the man was her father.

231

"I don't know, baby." She tucked a strand of Kenzie's hair behind her ear. "You were very brave. We're safe now."

Ms. Carmen eyed the half-prepared lasagna. "Care if I order pizza?"

Relief flooded Mama's face. "That would be nice. Thank you."

Thirty minutes later, the four of them watched a movie while they ate. When Kenzie fell asleep, Bronwyn lifted her sister and carried her into the bedroom. She tucked Annalise under Kenzie's arm.

"I have a friend who is a defense lawyer," Bronwyn overheard Ms. Carmen. "He specializes in domestic violence cases."

Mama exhaled. "My husband is too powerful."

"Then it's time he met his match." Ms. Carmen touched Mama's hand. "Let me call my friend."

Bronwyn took a seat. "We can't keep running, Mama."

The silence magnified the earlier conflict.

"You're right." Mama brushed her fingers against her cheek. "It's time to fight back."

Bronwyn had waited so long to hear those words. Could they really win?

Ms. Carmen read her thoughts. "You're stronger than you think."

Bronwyn gulped. Then why did she feel so afraid?

A long week passed before the news finally came.

Porter was alive. As soon as we learned he was out of critical condition, a jumble of texts and messages jammed Mom's phone. Guard families could all breathe easier. Our soldier would make it home.

The doctors couldn't save Porter's left leg below the knee, but his remarkable recovery was nothing short of a miracle. Emotion clouded the Maj's voice when he called us. The roller coaster of emotions had been tough for all the soldiers.

Three weeks later, Porter was headed home to his wife and kids where he'd begin a new battle— learning how to adjust to life with a prosthesis.

I sat on my bike and fingered the key which had been inside the final envelope labeled "legacy." The coordinates led me to a fork in a gravel road two miles from our house. The Maj had instructed me not to read the letter until I stood at the crossroads.

Dear Teegan,

My deepest hope is that I'm on an airplane headed home as you read these words. But life is unpredictable. There are no guarantees we will be reunited at the end of my deployment.

This treasure hunt is my legacy to you. The key you hold in your hands is a symbol.

You stand at a crossroads each day, facing decisions that will impact your future as well as those around you.

What will you choose? How will you live?

Each treasure holds a key on how to live each day.

Miracles. Dare. Together. Death. Regret. Procrastination. Catalyst. Distractions. Courage. Passion. Anyway. Legacy.

If nothing more, I hope this treasure hunt has taught you not to count down the days until my return, but rather to count the opportunities in each day.

You are my legacy, and I will always be with you.

Love, Dad

I refolded the note as memories from the last year of Jada, little Charlie, Grammie, and Cardboard City flooded my mind. The Maj had taught me to see past my own fears and focus on others through his yearlong treasure hunt. It wasn't easy—not when soldiers got attacked, and life could be a land mine of panic attacks and fear. But the Maj wanted me to live despite the unknowns.

My dad couldn't have left a better legacy.

***

Mom checked her make-up for the fourth time in the mirror on the back of the visor. Good thing Colter was driving, or we'd get in a car wreck before we made it to the welcome home ceremony.

"Nervous?" I sat on my hands to stop the tremble. The countdown had reached the final hour. The Maj and his soldiers were within the last miles of home.

"Extremely," she exhaled.

"Me, too," I admitted. A year was a long time.

Colter squeezed Mom's hand. "It's over."

"Look at all the people." Grandma leaned forward from the back seat and gaped out of the window. Poppy was silent beside her, the past no doubt replaying in his mind.

I stared through the glass to read the well wishes on every business marquee we passed. Yellow ribbons adorned electrical poles along the convoy route. A lump lodged in my throat from all the people who lined the streets holding homemade welcome home signs. The whole town had shown up to cheer on our soldiers.

Thank you for your service.

We're proud of our soldiers.

Welcome home to the red, white, and blue.

Each sign was a love letter from our country.

A low rumble grew louder as we approached the armory. Bikers decked out in black leather formed a protective barrier around the perimeter with their motorcycles. Two dozen volunteers from the Patriot Guard Riders reeved their bikes to salute us as we made our way to the parking lot with the other families. Many had been veterans themselves like Poppy where the homecoming hadn't been warm or welcoming.

Patriotic music blared from a sound system. The last minutes ticked by in electric excitement. Flags waved everywhere I looked.

"Look. There's Charlie." I touched Mom's sleeve when I spotted him and Katrina in the crowd. He kicked his legs in her arms and grasped a little flag in his fist.

Katrina caught my eye and waved. She looked radiant in a fitted red dress.

The blast of a horn signaled their arrival. Two blue military buses pulled into the lot. Soldiers stuck their heads out of open windows and waved. Cheers erupted like fireworks around me.

I craned my neck to see the Maj, but he was lost in a sea of camouflage. When he exited the first bus, my heart soared at the first glimpse of him.

Mom and I took off running. I jumped into his arms first and felt his strong embrace. His rugged scent mixed with the faintest whiff of his cologne filled my lungs.

"You're here," I cried into his neck. "You're really here."

I didn't want to let go.

Ever.

My dad was finally home. For good.

***

Teegan found me in the crowd as we made our way inside the armory for the homecoming ceremony. The other girls circled around me. Bing suffocated me with her usual exuberant hug. Her welcome home poster looked like a display from an art gallery.

"Congratulations." Hoot squeezed my hand.

"We're so happy for you." Mia beamed.

The MC tapped the microphone, directing people to take their seats.

"I feel like I'm dreaming." My voice squeaked as we found seats in the second row. "I can't believe he's really home."

Teegan's smile reached her ears. "There's more good news." She thrust a letter toward me.

I raised an eyebrow as the girls stared at me in collective anticipation.

"Who's this from?" I turned the envelope over in my hand and noticed the return address.

"It's from Bronwyn." Teegan's eyes shone.

"What?" I stuttered, scanning the words in disbelief. We'd only heard from Bronwyn once, and that was over a year ago.

Hey Girls,

It's me. Can you believe it?

So much has happened. I don't know where to start. Life hasn't been easy. We've been living on the streets.

But we're finally safe. And we have a real home. Mama is teaching, and we don't have to run anymore. He's finally in jail—where he'll be for a long time, according to the lawyer.

I can live again. Mama is smiling, and Kenzie can't stop giggling.

Please write back. I can't wait to hear all the news.

Love ya,
Bronwyn

Relief washed over me. The monster was locked up. I felt like shouting and dancing and running all at once.

"She's safe," Teegan whispered as the room quieted.

I choked back my tears. Bronwyn and Kenzie didn't have to run anymore. Their nights sleeping at a homeless shelter were over.

The Maj wasn't the only one home.

Bronwyn and Kenzie were finally home, too.

***

"Your mom rocks," Hoot exclaimed, and the girls murmured their agreement. "I can't believe she hired a seamstress to make you a camouflage formal for the kids' military ball."

"How else would she have gotten Rooster in a dress?" Mia laughed. She was in her element, surrounded by hair products and makeup.

They circled around me in front of the long mirror in my room, and we all stared at my image, somewhat dumbfounded. Olive green spaghetti straps stood out against my too-white skin while a fitted bodice showed my nonexistent curves. The skirt fell just above my knobby knees. The last time I wore a dress I was missing my two front teeth.

"Only you could pull off combat boots." Teegan eyed my choice of footwear. "But somehow it fits."

"If you can convince your mom." Bing pointed to my open closet. "Aren't those the shoes she bought?"

I frowned at the black wedges on the floor. Agreeing to wear the dress was torture enough. Add heels, and I wouldn't leave my room.

"Sit down." Mia waved her spiral curling iron wand in the air. "You promised I could curl your hair."

I groaned. "It looks fine."

"Fine isn't good enough." She pushed me into a chair. "We're going for masterpiece."

Ugh. I'd rather be outside tearing it up on the ATV.

"Relax." Mia wrapped a hank of hair around the wand. "It won't kill you to get pampered for once."

"That's debatable," I muttered.

Bing and Hoot each took a hand to add fingernail polish. They promised me camouflage.

"Beautiful." Mia unwound the first curl.

I frowned. "It's too springy."

Mia spun me around so I couldn't see the mirror. "Don't be such a critic. I'm just getting started."

"How long is this going to take?"

"An hour, tops."

"An hour?" I slumped over.

"Sit up." Mia ignored my complaints and took another section of hair. "Or you'll get burned."

The minutes passed in agonizing slowness. Mia enjoyed my pain too much.

I rubbed the sleep from my eyes when she finally turned me toward the mirror. At least she didn't force me to wear make-up.

"So, what do you think?" Mia held her breath.

The girl staring back looked like me, only way too girly. If it wasn't for the camouflage, I would've locked myself in my room.

"Wow," Bing muttered. "You just inspired my next painting."

Hoot whistled. "You look beautiful."

239

"The Maj is going to have the best looking date at the ball," Teegan echoed.

I managed a weak smile. My friends were trying to help, and Mia looked so hopeful, I didn't want to crush them. "Thanks, guys."

Mia grabbed the hairspray.

"No." I held out my hand before she could drench me in a sticky cloud. "This is as good as I get."

She only pouted for a few seconds, then grinned. "Come on, let's go show you off to the Maj."

I inhaled at the top of the stairs. Good thing I was wearing combat boots. Otherwise, I'd stumble toward the bottom with all the grace of an elephant trying to do ballet.

"Wow." The Maj looked up at me and whistled. He was dressed in his full dress blues. A rainbow of award ribbons decorated the front of his jacket.

Heat burned my face. All eyes on me on the basketball court was one thing. All eyes on me in a dress was a completely different manner.

"Go." Mia nudged me forward with her hip.

I gripped the railing and managed to descend the stairs in one piece.

Mom lowered the camera in her hand. "You look beautiful, Josie."

I grabbed her neck in a surprise embrace. She wrapped her arms around me and didn't let go.

"Thanks." I gulped back a sudden rush of emotion as the challenges of the past year gushed to the forefront of my memory. Through it all, my mom never wavered. Day after difficult day, she was there for me. "For everything."

Another set of arms enveloped us both. Strong arms accompanied a deep voice. "It's good to be home." The Maj kissed the top of my head and then brushed Mom's lips with a kiss.

"Aww." Bing jumped into the middle. "Come on, girls. Group hug."

A tangle of bodies invaded our private family moment, hemming us into a tighter circle. Warm breath touched my skin. Across from me, Teegan's head touched mine, and her eyes twinkled when our gaze met across the pocket of space. The Maj was finally home. Safe and alive and here in this moment. I couldn't help but grin.

Loud sniffles broke the spell. The circle disbanded leaving Bing clinging to my arm.

Mia couldn't pry her off me, so Teegan tickled her.

Bing's squeals only encouraged the rest of us.

The Maj went for me, and soon an all-out tickle war erupted. When we finally called a truce, my sides hurt from laughing so hard.

If only countries could avoid real war with a tickle war instead, the world would be a whole lot happier.

***

Silver balloons and purple streamers decorated the drill floor at the armory. Confetti sprinkled tables covered with white linen tablecloths while music played in the background.

A popcorn and candy bar attracted a handful of younger kids in frilly dresses and dress pants and ties. Several teens hung out on the outskirts eyeing the colored popcorn and candy like me. The organizers from the family support center knew just how to get kids excited.

241

"Josie?" A familiar voice made me turn.

Katrina glowed in a shimmering silver evening dress. Her husband held little Charlie who wore small black pants and a onesie with a printed tuxedo tie.

"Look at you." I marveled at Charlie. He'd doubled in weight since his days in the NICU.

Katrina gazed up at her husband with the same look of adoration I saw in my mom's eyes. Relief and peace replaced the shadow of anxiety and fear.

"Isn't this fun?" Katrina looked around the room. "What a fun idea to honor military kids."

The Maj took Charlie in his big hands. "You should be proud, young man. Your dad served our country well. I'm sure you'll follow in his footsteps someday."

Harrison straightened and saluted the Maj. "It was an honor to serve alongside you, sir."

The Maj excused himself to talk to other soldiers and their families. Watching him made me proud. The mutual respect between the soldiers and their commander was obvious.

A soldier limped up to the Maj. He held hands with a toddler wearing a frilly dress. She hid behind his artificial leg and gave a shy smile.

"Good to see you, sir." He favored his right leg when he saluted my father.

"Sergeant major." The Maj stood to attention, and his eyes misted. "You look great. How're you adjusting to your new leg?"

"It's a battle all in itself, sir." The sergeant major's jaw tightened. "But the physical therapists are all treating me good. And my wife has been a rock." He eyed a lady in a black dress talking with two other women. "I couldn't do it without her."

The Maj put an arm around my shoulder. "Well said, soldier. Our families mean everything." He smiled at the sergeant major's daughter. "She can be proud of her daddy. I know I'm proud to have served with you."

The sergeant major tried to speak, but emotion overcame him. We made our way to our table, and I slipped my hand into the Maj's hand—something I rarely did anymore—and his surprise turned to a smile.

Before the speaker took the stage, the MC directed the attention of the audience to a lone table next to a POW/MIA flag.

Emotion welled inside me. I was not alone. Sniffles peppered the crowd. The smaller table symbolized the frailty of one prisoner against his or her oppressors while a black napkin stood for the emptiness experienced by family and friends. Salt on the bread plate represented the tears shed, an inverted wine glass symbolized absence, and a yellow candle and ribbon equaled everlasting hope for a joyous reunion.

I eyed the Maj and prayed a silent prayer of gratitude that he and his unit had made it home. Not one soldier was left behind.

The chaplain blessed the kid friendly food—chicken strips and gourmet mac and cheese—before the speaker took the stage and had us all laughing.

"Want to get our picture before the dance?" The Maj led me to the photo area where one of the family support workers encouraged us to grab props.

"We'll do a silly shot first." She pointed to a collection of props. "Then a formal picture."

The Maj selected some Groucho Marx glasses, and I flung a neon pink boa around my neck.

"Cheese!" The Maj grabbed me and surprised me with a dip.

The DJ got everyone to the dance floor with a line-up of interactive songs including the "Cha-Cha Slide," and the "Cotton-Eyed Joe." We laughed at a kid who tore up the dance floor, oblivious to the video cameras recording him. The kid was good enough to be the next YouTube sensation.

The music switched to a slower tempo, and the Maj asked me to dance.

I wasn't much for dancing in front of an audience, but the Maj was persuasive. At least the dim lights would hide my lack of coordination.

I leaned into his chest, and the sound of his heartbeat helped me relax. Lee Greenwood's song "Proud to be an American" played over the speakers, bringing a throng to the dance floor. Watching soldier dads with their little girls and moms in uniforms with their sons made me stop. It was a rare moment—precious after a year of separation—and I wanted to remember every detail. Freedom wasn't free.

"Have you thought much about your birthday trip?" the Maj asked when another song started.

I'd spent hours thinking about our trip together. Backpacking in the Rockies, snorkeling in the ocean, hiking down the Grand Canyon—an adventure with the Maj would be fun anywhere. "Do you care if I invite someone?"

"How many someones are we talking about?" Curiosity sparkled in his eyes. "The whole basketball team?"

I flashed a winning smile. "Just the starting lineup and Bronwyn."

"Six teenage girls?" The Maj exhaled. "How will I survive?"

"You survived Afghanistan, didn't you?"

The Maj chuckled. "Sounds like a challenge to me."

I crossed my fingers. "So, do you accept?"

The Maj twirled me around. "Game on."

***

Bronwyn packed the last of her clothes and closed her bag. She was tempted to read Oliver's note, but he made her promise that she wouldn't open it until after she left. A smile touched her lips. Somehow Oliver had made his way into her heart.

The girls would be at the apartment any minute. Bronwyn couldn't wait for all the fun they'd have. She was actually taking a real vacation with her best friends. Bronwyn could only imagine the junk food they'd eat. Twizzlers, Oreos, Pringles, peanut M&Ms, Easy Cheese and crackers—they each had their favorites. A lot had happened since their last junk food potluck on the bus ride home after a middle school basketball game.

"How long will you be gone again?" Kenzie sat on the edge of her bed holding Annalise.

"Five days." She took a seat, and her sister snuggled closer.

"I'll miss you."

"I'll be home sooner than you know." Bronwyn smiled. She didn't want her sister to see her own hesitation. After everything they'd been through, leaving Mama and Kenzie was harder than Bronwyn imagined. She hadn't slept more than an hour between her nerves and excitement.

245

"Will you send me a postcard?" Kenzie lit up. *"I've always wanted a postcard."*

"Everyday."

"And bring me back a souvenir?"

Bronwyn hooked her pinkie with Kenzie's and promised.

A horn blared through the open window.

"They're here." She jumped up and grabbed her bag. *"The girls are really here."*

Five sets of arms enveloped Bronwyn. Six heads touched, their hair meshing together. Bronwyn stared at the faces inside the huddle, and she was back with her friends on the basketball court.

For the briefest moment, no one broke the sacred silence as memories and relief washed over them.

Bronwyn was safe.

The girls were together again.

Sneak Peek from *Fearless*
Book Three: The Anonymous Chronicles

Prologue
June 2013

Spindly tree limbs creaked in the wind. Their eerie shadows spread across the canvas tent like ominous tentacles ready to curl around Bronwyn's neck and strangle her. A woeful howl rose above the drone of insects, making goosebumps blotch her flesh.

Bronwyn buried herself deep inside her sleeping bag only to feel the suffocating weight press against her thudding heart. Nights exaggerated her fears. Ever since Mama called with the news, Bronwyn had gotten little sleep. Her father had posted bail.

Dilated brown pupils searched the dark. The rhythmic breathing of her friends did little to soothe Bronwyn. She kicked herself for leaving Mama and Kenzie to go to Jackson Hole, Wyoming. Agreeing to join her friends on a camping trip had been a mistake—even if she hadn't seen the girls in over a year and a half.

Mama had filed a temporary restraining order against her father, but he was too powerful. What if he came after them? Bronwyn needed to go home. A 12-hour drive separated her from her mother and little sister.

She'd never forgive herself if he hurt them.

The walls of the tent threatened to smother Bronwyn. She had to escape.

Bronwyn slipped out of the nest of warmth and sidestepped the jumbled knot of legs and arms. Careful not to make noise, she unzipped the door on the tent and stepped outside.

Cool mountain air filled Bronwyn's lungs as she stared at an indigo sky pierced with innumerable stars. A shooting star streaked the surface. Out here—away from the monster—she could almost relax and forget her fears.

The chill demanded a blanket, but Bronwyn didn't want to wake her friends. She padded toward the fire ring and sat on a lawn chair, hugging her knees to conserve body heat.

A tendril of smoke rose from the dying embers. Roasting marshmallows had been an adventure with Bing. The girl should be banned from fire. She was an accident waiting to happen.

Thoughts of her friends always brought a smile. Bronwyn had met Bing, Teegan, Mia, Hoot, and Rooster during try-outs on the middle school basketball court. Despite her attempt to distance herself, Bronwyn couldn't help but love the girls.

She didn't want to ruin the trip for her friends, but what choice did she have? Mama and Kenzie needed her.

Bronwyn exhaled, and the puff of air condensed in a small cloud. Rooster would be disappointed. This camping trip had been a gift from the Maj after his deployment to Afghanistan. Rooster could've chosen to do anything with her dad, and she'd invited the girls.

Bronwyn had never been on a real vacation. Life on the run didn't allow for distractions. She didn't want to miss white river rafting, but at least they'd already been rock climbing and fly fishing. Bronwyn even caught a fish the first time she'd snapped the line into the current.

Anger threatened to choke her airway. Why did he always have to ruin everything?

Bronwyn wanted to scream.
Would she ever be free to live a normal life?

Chapter One
June 2013

I didn't want to be the chicken in the group. But my brain wouldn't stop replaying all the YouTube videos I'd watched before our trip.

Rafts overturning.

People flying overboard.

Or my personal favorite—the guide explaining the waiver you had to sign regarding the dangers inherent in white water river rafting. Why would any sane person agree to sign his or her death certificate?

I, for one, did not have a fatal wish.

Rooster and Teegan lived for this type of thrill, Bing was oblivious to danger, Hoot wouldn't rock the boat (pun intended), and Bronwyn was too distracted with bigger worries to concern herself with dying. Just convincing her to stay on the trip for our remaining 24 hours together had been a minor miracle after her father had posted bail.

I hopped out of the minivan the Maj had rented for our motley group and followed the others inside the outfitters.

Breathe in, Mia. Breathe out.

I had to talk myself out of a full blown panic attack when the river guide briefed us on safety.

Bronwyn stood off to the side, a haunted look in her eyes.

"You okay?" I pushed my fears aside and tried to put myself in her shoes. She and her mother and sister had tried to escape her father for over five years. His recent arrest had finally brought relief until an incompetent judge released him on bail.

Didn't the guy wielding the gavel read the police report? Bronwyn's father had pulled a knife on her mother. The unfairness was enough to persuade me to study law rather than fashion design. The injustice infuriated me.

"The Maj called his friend on the police force," I tried to reassure Bronwyn. "There's nothing you can do for your mother and Kenzie."

Tears welled her eyes. "I should be home with them."

"You will be." I squeezed Bronwyn's hand. "We leave tomorrow morning."

Loading the outfitters' bus ended our conversation and kicked my brain into overdrive once again.

The rapids on the Snake River were classified as class II-III rapids during normal water conditions, but researching the description of class V-VI rapids had been a mistake. My memory was practically photographic when it came to details such as "rescue conditions are difficult" or "warning: significant hazard to life can result in the event of a mishap." Terror ignited my nerves.

I gripped the seat when the bus pulled to a stop. My throat contracted to a pinhole.

Breathe in. Breathe out.

The sound of water made my heart race. The guide promised the first half of the trip was fairly mellow, but that didn't stop my ears from magnifying the sound of gurgling water to a rushing torrent of trepidation.

I tried not to think about jagged rocks below the surface and secured my life jacket.

Breathe in. Breathe out.

The Maj helped the guide unload the bright yellow raft, and I strapped on my helmet.

Rooster whistled at my life jacket/helmet ensemble. "Work it, girl."

I stuck out my tongue. I'd forgo fashion any day to save my skull from getting dashed on the rocks. Of course Rooster had her own wetsuit. The girl could pose for the cover of an outdoor magazine.

"You ready for this?" Hoot smiled, making me envy her ability to relax. I felt like I could hurl. The Maj's gourmet outdoor breakfast of pancakes and bacon settled like a rock in my stomach.

Bing waded at the river's edge in her water shoes, so Teegan grabbed her before she did a face-plant into the water.

"We need a selfie." Hoot pulled out her phone, and the others squeezed together. "Come on, Mia."

I took a tentative step, sure my wobbly legs would give way. Tanning beside a pool trumped rushing rapids. How had my friends ever convinced me to join their insanity?

"Let me take it." The Maj took Hoot's phone, and five more hands jutted out. "Can you take one for me, too?"

I slipped beside Bronwyn, happy to see the smile which finally graced her face. I inhaled. If she could be brave, so could I.

Teegan and Rooster slapped hands. "This is going to be so fun."

I forced a smile as another raft launched into the river. Two kids waved from the center, their laughter filling the air. One thing was certain: this adventure would definitely be one for the memory books.

"You okay?" Hoot squeezed my hand.

I couldn't look at the selfies, sure my face was a sickly green. "Fine," I squeaked as we boarded the raft.

My friends grabbed oars and took the front seats, but I planted myself firmly in the middle as close to the guide as possible. No paddling for me.

"Any final questions?" he asked before we pushed off. I couldn't even focus on the cute dimple that showed when he smiled.

One question pressed against my chest, making breathing nearly impossible.

Was I going to die?

About the Author

A group of middle school students who read an early draft of *Nameless* encouraged Angela to write *Faceless*. Wanting to know more of Bronwyn's story, they begged her to write another book. Angela's first trilogy was born out of that request with *Fearless* to follow in 2017. Angela's husband, an officer in the National Guard, inspired the Maj. Another soldier and his wife became the model for Harrison and Katrina when Angela helped in the delivery room with their twins. These pages are her tribute to the many sacrifices made by military members and their families.

When she is not writing or reading, Angela loves to jet ski, travel, swim, bike (especially tandem with her husband), and spend time with her family. Summers are spent volunteering with Teen Reach Adventure Camp, a biblically-based camp for teens residing in foster care. A portion of *Faceless* will help more teens attend camp.

As an indie writer, Angela strives for excellence. Without the backing of a big publisher, however, she relies on word of mouth. Please tell your friends and share your feedback on Amazon or Goodreads by writing a short review. Also look for Angela's other young adult titles: *BRAiN RIDE*, *Late Summer Monarch*, *Tandem*, and *Nameless*. Contact the author, or find out more at www.angelawelchprusia.com.

Acknowledgments

Soli Deo Gloria. For God's glory alone.

Will. I love you more with every passing day. It's no wonder you show up in every book.

Blake, Meghan, & Keely. Life is rich because of you three. Be the difference.

Dad & Mom. I inherited my love for books from you. Thanks for encouraging me to dream.

I'm so grateful to so many others.

Chelsea Kuhl, amazing proofreader.

Early draft reader and gifted basketball player Vanessa Leeper Jones and Westside Middle School beta readers, Elsie McCabe, Ariana Dykhouse, Abigail Carlson, and Brandon Wigodsky.

Crowdspring.com for your team of talented graphic artists and cover designer, Craig Granger.

56285142R00147

Made in the USA
Charleston, SC
14 May 2016